LAMBS IN THE LANE

'Mandy, stop the bike,' James cried. 'Look!'

'What is it? What's wrong?' Mandy stopped the quad bike abruptly.

'That battered old pick-up,' said James. 'I don't think the driver knows the sheep are there. He keeps slowing down and then speeding up again.'

They watched helplessly as the pick-up truck disappeared from view behind the hedge where the road bent sharply round the corner of the field. There was a dreadful screech of brakes, a thud, then the tinkling sound of breaking glass. For a moment there was absolute silence, then all that could be heard was the bleating of terrified sheep . . .

Animal Ark series

Plus:
Little Animal Ark
Animal Ark Pets
Animal Ark Hauntings
Animal Ark Holiday Specials

LUCY DANIELS

Lambs
— in the —
Lane

Illustrations by Ann Baum

Hodder
Children's
Books

a division of Hodder Headline Limited

**For Edna, Cath and the real Rebecca
at Hazel Brow Farm**

Special thanks to Tanis Jordan

**Thanks also to C. J. Hall, B.Vet.Med., M.R.C.V.S., for reviewing
the veterinary information contained in this book.**

Animal Ark is a trademark of Working Partners Limited
Text copyright © 2003 Working Partners Limited
Created by Working Partners Limited, London W6 0QT
Original series created by Ben M. Baglio
Illustrations copyright © 2003 Ann Baum

First published in Great Britain in 2003
by Hodder Children's Books

For more information about Animal Ark,
please contact www.animalark.co.uk

10 9 8 7 6 5 4 3 2 1

A Catalogue record for this book is available from
the British Library

ISBN 0 340 87387 6

Typeset by Avon Dataset Ltd, Bidford-on-Avon, Warks

Printed and bound in Great Britain by
Clays Ltd, St Ives plc

The paper and board used in this paperback by
Hodder Children's Books are natural recyclable products made from
wood grown in sustainable forests. The manufacturing processes
conform to the environmental regulations of the country of origin.

Hodder Children's Books
a division of Hodder Headline Limited
338 Euston Road
London NW1 3BH

One

'Don't forget these!' Adam Hope called as Mandy and her best friend, James Hunter, jumped eagerly from the Land-rover and ran towards the gate of Syke Farm.

Mandy Hope stopped in her tracks and turned round. Her dad was leaning out of the window, a couple of bike helmets dangling from his hand.

'You know it makes sense,' Mr Hope grinned. 'Those quad bikes are capable of high speeds and we don't want any accidents, do we?'

Mandy smiled back. 'We'll be careful, Dad,' she

promised, taking the helmets and dashing back to join James.

'I'll bring your lunch over later,' he called after her. Mandy waved as the Land-rover pulled away down the lane. Mandy's parents were vets and ran a successful practice called Animal Ark in the nearby village of Welford. Adam Hope was going back to oversee Saturday morning surgery while Mandy and James were at Syke Farm.

Mandy followed James through the gate, shutting it carefully behind her. 'Gran's making us a picnic,' she said, watching with a grin as James's eyes lit up at the thought of the tempting sandwiches and homemade cake that her gran was famous for. 'First though,' she added, 'we've got to work to earn it!'

They glanced round the yard, which was edged with low, grey stone buildings. At first it seemed deserted, then they heard voices coming from the barn and a woman emerged. She was short and thin and dressed in old brown trousers tucked into black rubber boots. Her green sweatshirt was faded and the sleeves were rolled up to the elbow. Her face and hands were weather-beaten from years of working outside all year round.

'You're back for more, then?' she greeted Mandy and James. 'You're not afraid of hard work, I'll say that for you.'

Dora Janeki owned Syke Farm, an isolated sheep farm high in the Yorkshire Dales, which she ran with the help of her brother, Ken Hudson. Most of their sheep spent the winter grazing up on the moors. These particular sheep were a tough breed with thick coats that kept out the rain and snow. But now spring had arrived, and the time had come to round them up and bring them down nearer to the farm in readiness for lambing. Mandy and James had jumped at the chance to help out during their school holidays.

'Ken's in the lambing field,' Dora told them, nodding in the direction of the field they had put the sheep in the day before. 'Some of those you brought down the other day are almost ready to lamb. You did well getting them down in the trailer.'

Mandy blushed with pride. Dora was very sparing with praise, and she was more likely to tell them what they were doing wrong, than what they had done right. Moving the first batch of sheep had been very hard work. They'd had to round them up from the very top of the moor, high up among the deep heather, with just two sheepdogs and Ken to help. The sheep were scattered over a large area, and tended to run off as soon as anyone approached. They didn't get to see many people up on the moors! Mandy thought they were almost as timid as rabbits or deer. It was all she and James could do to gather the sheep together and herd them safely into the trailer. Finally Mandy and James had squeezed into the tractor cab with Ken to drive down the track to the farm, hanging on tightly as the vehicle bounced in and out of huge potholes caused by the severe winter weather.

'Ken said we could use the quad to bring down the rest of the sheep,' Mandy told Dora, looking round the yard to see if she could spot the bright green four-wheeled motorbike.

'So he did,' Dora agreed, a smile creasing her face. 'You won't find it here though. He's already taken it up for you. You aren't allowed to ride it on the road, remember.'

'We'd better get up there then!' Mandy said. 'Ken might be waiting for us.'

'Make sure you check the gullies well,' Dora instructed as she walked with them to the gate. 'Sheep are crafty – they like to hide away in them. And some of the ewes in this flock have minds of their own!'

'OK, we will,' Mandy promised as she and James set off up the lane.

Mandy sniffed the air. Everything smelled fresh in the new green of spring. The dale was quiet except for the distant bleating of sheep coming from the sides of the valley.

'First one there gets to drive,' Mandy shouted, breaking into a run. She was almost at the lambing field when she heard James's footsteps coming up behind her. There was a clang as they both flung themselves at the metal gate.

'Tie!' James panted, gasping for breath.

Mandy spotted Ken on the far side of the field and waved, then stood holding her sides, getting her breath back.

'You'll be tired before you've even started,' Ken joked, coming over. He opened the gate and stepped through into the lane. 'I've left the bike up in the next field. I didn't want to worry these ewes by bringing it in here. Some of them look as if they might drop their lambs any moment!'

They walked up the lane until they came to a double-barred gate just before a sharp bend. Through the bars, Mandy could see the shiny quad bike, glinting in the morning sunshine. She felt a thrill of anticipation. She'd often ridden behind Ken, but she'd never had the chance to drive on her own. They clambered over the gate while Ken stood watching.

'Please can you bring those sheep down from the next field and let them gather at this gate,' said Ken, glancing at his watch. 'It shouldn't take you more than an hour and a half. I'll come back with the dogs at midday and we'll move them across the road.' He frowned up at the sky. 'There's bad weather forecast for today, so we'll need to get them in as soon as we can.'

'Right,' Mandy said, putting on her helmet and tightening the strap.

'The bike is very easy to ride,' Ken told them. 'You've seen me drive enough times, so I know you'll be fine. Just don't try to go too fast, especially where the ground's a bit bumpy. Don't want you tipping over! Who's driving first?'

Mandy and James looked at each other. 'We can't decide,' James confessed.

'Toss for it,' Ken suggested. He took a coin from his pocket and threw it in the air.

'Heads!' James cried as the coin landed on the ground.

Ken bent down to pick it up. 'Sorry, James,' he commiserated, 'tails it is.' He handed the key to Mandy. 'There you go. Swap over after three-quarters of an hour, why don't you?'

Mandy climbed on the bike and started it up, just as she had seen Ken do before. She gently squeezed the accelerator lever under her thumb to rev the engine. James climbed on to the seat behind her, holding Mandy's shoulders tightly as she cautiously set off up the hill.

Mandy thought the bike was fantastic. Once she'd got the feel of it, she changed gear by flipping the lever under her right foot. The bike jerked a bit, then accelerated smoothly away. Mandy steered the bike along the track at the edge of the field, being careful to avoid the potholes. At the far side of the field, there was a gate that led on to the open moor. The stony track gave way to coarse, close-cropped grass, dotted with clumps of heather and smooth grey boulders. Mandy drove slowly along the ridge, checking for any stray sheep.

'Over there!' James shouted behind her, pointing down into a shallow valley where several white bodies were busy grazing.

Mandy nodded and steered the quad bike down

into the dip, taking the longest route so that she could get behind the flock. Slowly she moved across the moor, back towards the gate, gathering sheep in front of the bike. The woolly rumps bobbed and bounced ahead, jumping over the heather and letting out nervous bleats if they thought the bike was getting too close. Once or twice, a particularly skittish ewe broke away, and Mandy had to steer the bike in a wide arc to shepherd it back to the rest of the flock. She became so engrossed in her job that at first she didn't notice James urgently tapping her shoulder.

'What's wrong?' she asked, cutting the engine and turning round.

'I think it's my turn,' he said in a pained voice, jumping down from the back.

Mandy looked at her watch. She could hardly believe it. She had gone way over the agreed forty-five minutes. She'd been driving for nearly an hour!

When James took over, Mandy found it was almost as much fun to ride pillion. She had a great view of the moors that stretched out on either side, and soon spotted a couple of sheep peering out from a gully just below them. Shaking James's shoulder, she pointed them out and he steered towards them. The ewes just wriggled further into the heather when they heard the quad coming. James parked the bike so that they could chase them out on foot and send them down to join the others.

Mandy and James worked solidly all morning, moving the sheep further and further down the moor towards the gate. It was hot and tiring, but they daren't stop for too long in case a ewe took the chance to make a break for it.

James brought the bike to a halt by the gate that led into the first field. 'Your turn,' he said, twisting round and grinning at Mandy.

Mandy jumped off and stared into the distance, shading her eyes from the sun. Deep in the valley, she could see a vehicle winding its way up to the moor. 'Look, James,' she observed. 'That's Dad, isn't it?'

James followed her gaze as he climbed off the bike. 'Yep,' he agreed. 'That's the Animal Ark Land-rover, you can't mistake it. I hope he's coming up here with our lunch. I'm starving!'

Mandy looked at her watch. 'Goodness, where's the morning gone?' she exclaimed. 'We'd better get a move on. Look, Ken's just come in the gate by the road.'

She climbed on the bike, and James hopped up behind her. Then they were off again, urging the sheep across the field to Ken. With a series of shrill whistles, he sent his two sheepdogs, Tess and Whistler, to help. With Mandy driving the sheep from the top of the hill and the dogs working on either side, the sheep were soon at the gate. Ken put up a hand to halt the bike and Mandy cut the engine. This was the tricky part – taking the sheep down to the lambing field on the other side of the lane. They just had to hope that no cars came along while the flock was on the move. Mandy's job now was to chase down any stragglers once the herd had begun crossing the road. She and James watched closely as Ken opened the gate and sent Whistler down the lane.

'Look, there's Charlie,' said James, pointing to the lower gate where Ken's assistant shepherd was waiting. Charlie hadn't been working at Syke

Farm for long, so Mandy had only met him a few times.

'It looks like Whistler's going to help him,' she said.

Ken propped open the gate and walked along to the bend in the road to keep an eye out for traffic. Mandy and James watched in admiration as Tess ran up and down in front of the sheep and kept the whole flock in the field until Ken gave a distinctive, two-toned whistle. Then Tess slipped away like a sleek black-and-white dart and allowed the flock to spill out of the gate. She raced round behind them and herded them down the lane to where Charlie was waiting.

Mandy started up the bike and drove behind, stopping the flock from turning back into the field. She could see that the sheep were pouring down the lane and through the gate into the lambing field. But then the sheep at the front stopped moving and began jostling one another with high-pitched, anxious bleats. Slowly Mandy drove the bike back up the hill to give the sheep space, and looked down at the scene below. It seemed that one or two of the ewes had spooked at something by the gate and the rest of the flock couldn't move forward, jumbling themselves up in the lane.

'I think we've got a traffic jam,' Mandy joked, as Ken jogged down the road and gave the front ewes a gentle prod with his shepherd's crook. She released the brake and started to head back down to the flock.

'Mandy, stop the bike!' James cried. 'Look!'

'What is it? What's wrong?' Mandy stopped the bike so abruptly that James lost his balance and fell off backwards.

'That battered old pick-up,' said James, scrambling to his feet and pointing to a truck coming along the valley in the opposite direction to the Land-rover. 'I don't think the driver knows the sheep are there. He keeps slowing down and then speeding up again.'

'He's getting near the bend.' Mandy felt her voice strain. At the gate, Ken was bent over the ewes, trying to make them move into the field. He obviously hadn't heard the approaching truck.

Mandy jumped off the bike and began waving her arms in the air. 'KEN, LOOK OUT!' she shouted at the top of her voice. 'KEN, THERE'S A CAR COMING!'

'Mandy!' exclaimed James, clutching hold of her arm. 'It's too late!'

They watched helplessly as the pick-up truck disappeared from view behind the hedge where the road bent sharply round the corner of the field. There was a dreadful screech of brakes, a thud, then the tinkling sound of breaking glass. For a moment there was absolute silence, then all that could be heard was the bleating of terrified sheep . . .

Two

'Hang on tight, James,' said Mandy, revving the engine. 'We've got to get down there to help!'

She steered wide of the sheep so that she didn't frighten them even more, but brought the bike as near to the gate as possible. Then she and James scrambled off and ran as fast as they could. The sheep skittered away, making a corridor as James and Mandy pushed their way through to the gate. Some of the sheep bolted back up the hillside, but they couldn't worry about that now. The scene that met them in the lane made Mandy shiver with fright. Sheep were dashing about wildly, while the two sheepdogs tore round instinctively bringing the flock back together. Ken was frantically checking the animals for signs of injury. Panic had spread through the whole flock and Charlie was having trouble keeping the ewes in the lambing field as they surged back towards the gate.

The battered old truck was stuck on the edge of an overgrown ditch on the opposite side of the lane. Its nearside headlight was broken where it had struck a telegraph pole and steam hissed from the radiator. The door was open and the driver was struggling to pull himself out. Further down the lane, Mandy saw the Animal Ark Land-rover slewed to a halt, with the driver's door hanging open.

'Dad?' Mandy called, feeling a rush of fear. Surely the Land-rover couldn't have been involved in the accident as well?

'Mandy, James, where are you?'

Mandy breathed out with relief when she heard her father's voice. Carefully making her way through the frightened animals, she saw her father hurrying towards her.

'We're OK, Dad,' she called, waving.

'There you are,' said Adam Hope, sounding as relieved as Mandy felt. He put his arms round her. 'I heard the crash as I came up the lane so I just jumped out and ran.' Still holding her, Adam Hope stretched out to put a hand on James's shoulder. 'Are you sure you're all right, you two? You're both as white as a sheet.'

'We're fine, Dad,' Mandy reassured him. 'It was just a terrible shock.'

'We could see it was going to happen,' explained James. 'But there wasn't anything we could do.'

'Just so long as you're not hurt,' said Adam Hope. 'I think we should go and help the driver out. He's in trouble over there.'

Ken, his face red with fury, straightened up from the ewe he was examining and glared angrily at the driver. 'Trouble?' he muttered. 'I'll give him trouble.'

James reached the truck first and balancing precariously on the bank, offered the man his hand.

'No, lad, I'd just pull you in on top of me,' the driver said, puffing as he struggled to heave himself out.

'I'll hang on to you from this side, James,' suggested Mr Hope, getting hold of James's other arm and reaching out to the man as well. The old man clasped the hands they offered and with a huge effort, hauled himself up the bank.

'Are you hurt?' asked Mandy's dad.

'No,' the man replied, brushing down his blue overalls and straightening his flat cap which had been knocked sideways by the crash. 'No damage done, just a bit shook up.' Out of the corner of her eye, Mandy saw Ken bearing down on them, looking very angry.

'You stupid old fool,' Ken shouted. 'I'm holding you responsible for any damage to my sheep. In fact,' he wagged a finger in the man's face, 'I'm holding you responsible for any damage to anything!'

'Now just hold on a minute, if you'd . . .' the man began, but Ken cut him off.

'Don't you tell me to hold on,' Ken ranted. 'If you hadn't been driving so fast and had been looking where you were going, this would never have happened. In fact, I think the police should know about this.'

'Aye,' the man said, drawing himself up straight, his voice angry too. 'Perhaps they should!'

Mandy saw that Ken was taken aback by the man's agreement.

'As I was about to say before you interrupted,' the man went on firmly, 'if there had been a look-out on that blind bend, I wouldn't have nearly driven into your sheep and been forced to end up in this ditch.' He glowered at Ken who looked away as if he was trying to think of a suitable reply. 'It could have been a lot nastier than it was,' the man added, 'if I hadn't been driving so carefully.'

Mandy and James exchanged glances as they remembered the man's erratic driving. But Mandy knew the man did have a point; there hadn't been a look-out on the bend.

'Now then,' Adam Hope intervened. 'Look at it this way, nobody's been hurt. None of the sheep were hit, were they Ken?'

Ken shoved his hands deep in his pockets and shook his head. 'Not that I can see,' he admitted grudgingly.

'Then as far as I can tell, you were both a bit at fault but what happened was a genuine accident,'

Mr Hope went on in a level voice. 'So why don't you shake hands and we'll get these sheep into the field before anyone else comes along?'

Mandy smiled to herself. Sometimes her dad was such a diplomat. She watched as he offered the old man his mobile phone to call a garage.

'Mandy,' James nudged her. 'Look over there.' He nodded towards the back of the van. Pressed up against the tailgate of the truck, shunted there by the accident, was a large wicker basket. Mandy and James stepped forward to investigate.

'That looks like an animal basket,' Mandy whispered, staring intently at the basket.

Then she jumped. 'It moved! James, look at the basket. It's moving, isn't it?'

James's eyes widened behind his glasses and he nodded. 'There's something in there, an animal or something,' he agreed.

'And it's trying to get out,' Mandy guessed, leaning as close as she could to the basket. 'Look, the catch has come loose. Excuse me.' Mandy turned to attract the attention of the old man. 'Excuse me, but this basket seems to be . . .'

'Oh no,' gasped the old man. His face took on a look of horror and he rushed towards the back of the van with his arms outstretched. But he was too late. Whatever was inside pushed up the lid of the basket so that the catch fell out. Before anyone could do anything to stop it, the lid sprang open and bounced against the side of the truck. There was a flurry of activity and the noisy beating of wings. Mandy stared in astonishment as dozens and dozens of pigeons came tumbling out! They flew straight up into the sky where they began circling, high above the treetops.

'Well, I'll be blowed,' said Ken, rubbing his chin. Mr Hope frowned in confusion, as if someone had just played a practical joke on him. But then Mandy's eyes were drawn to the old man and her heart sank. His face began to crumple, the look of horror replaced by one of utter despair.

'My birds,' he said hopelessly. 'My very best birds. Gone.' Peering into the basket as if he hoped he might find one still there, he shook his head. 'All gone.'

Mandy felt so sorry for him, she went over and gently touched his arm. 'Are they special birds?' she asked softly.

'Aye,' the old man said in a weary voice. 'They're the pick of my racing pigeons. They're the best pigeons in Yorkshire. I was on my way to a show when this happened.' He waved his hand at the truck in the ditch.

'But won't they come back?' James asked.

The old man shook his head. 'Normally they would, the experienced ones, that is. But we're in for a storm, look at those clouds.'

Mandy scanned the far horizon. While they had been dealing with the accident, dark clouds had appeared and were now scudding across the sky. She remembered what Ken had said earlier that morning about the weather forecast.

'That'll upset them and put them right off-course.' The old man sighed deeply. 'I'd never race a bird in bad weather.'

Ken sniffed in agreement. 'A storm's definitely coming. We'd best get these sheep sorted, Charlie.' Before he turned away, he reached out and rather awkwardly patted the old man on the shoulder. 'I'm sorry about your birds,' he said. 'I wouldn't have wished that on you.'

'I know. I'll give you a hand with the sheep if you like,' the old man offered, 'while I'm waiting for the garage to take away my truck. There's nothing I can do about my pigeons now, anyway, except worry about them.'

'Thanks,' Ken replied gratefully. 'We could use all the help we can get.'

'My name's Harry Wainwright, by the way,' said the old man.

'Ken Hudson,' said Ken. 'And this is Mandy, and James, and Mandy's dad, Adam Hope.'

Harry nodded to them all, and managed to smile. 'Let's get going, then,' he said. 'We don't want any mishaps with these sheep.'

Working together with the dogs, they soon had all the strays rounded up and the entire flock safely in the lambing field. Helped by Mandy and James, Adam Hope had given the ewes a quick check as they trotted through the gate, just to be sure that none of them had gone into premature labour. After all, they'd had more excitement than was good for such heavily expectant mums! When

Charlie finally shut the gate, they breathed sighs of relief.

'It looks as if we've beaten the rain,' said Adam Hope cheerfully, then he changed his tone when he noticed Harry looking glum. 'I think it's time for lunch,' he suggested. 'There's a picnic in the Land-rover, if you'd like to join us, Mr Wainwright.'

Charlie, Ken's assistant shepherd, looked anxiously at the sky. 'I'd better get on,' he said to Ken. 'There's a fence needs mending in the lower pasture. Do you want me to leave one of the dogs with you?'

'No, take them both. I've finished here, I'll just do a final check then I'll be down for my lunch.'

'I must get my basket from the truck and some other bits and pieces, before the tow-truck arrives,' said Harry. 'What a day this has turned out to be. I don't think anything more could go wrong.'

'James and I will come and help you,' Mandy suggested.

'Come for a bite to eat in the Land-rover when

you've finished,' Adam Hope called out to them.

As they reached the truck, a car pulled up beside them.

'Is everything all right?' asked the driver, winding down his window.

'Yes, thanks, everything's under control now,' Mandy told him. 'It's kind of you to stop.'

'No problem,' the man replied. 'I know how dangerous these narrow lanes can be.'

He drove off, steering carefully round the bend and accelerating along the valley.

'Good job he wasn't here half an hour earlier,' joked James. 'He'd never have got through.'

'Hang on a minute,' Mandy said, holding up one hand. 'I can hear a funny sound.'

James listened. 'I can't hear anything,' he said.

'Nor me,' agreed Harry Wainwright. 'But then, my hearing's not what it used to be.'

Mandy concentrated hard. The sound was faint but it was definitely there. And with a feeling of dread, Mandy realised she knew what it was.

'I just heard it again. I think it's a sheep bleating,' she said urgently. 'I'm sure of it. James – quick, get Ken.'

But when Ken arrived at a run, James panting beside him, Mandy had to admit that she hadn't heard the sound again. For half a minute they stood in silence, listening, and then Ken turned to walk away.

'You've heard so many sheep bleating this morning, Mandy,' he said with a smile, 'I'm not surprised they're echoing in your head.'

Mandy gave him a wan smile in return. She didn't want to argue, but she knew what she'd heard. And then she heard it again. Glancing over at Ken, she saw the blood drain from his face. He'd obviously heard it, too.

'It's coming from under the truck!' he gasped. 'Do you think we can push it back a bit? It can't go forward because it's jammed against that telegraph pole.'

'We can try, but I put the handbrake on,' said Harry, looking worried. 'I'll have to get in to let it off.'

'No!' Ken exclaimed immediately. 'No more weight on the truck if we can help it.' He looked around for help. 'Mandy, you're the lightest. Do you think you could lean in and let the brake off?

We'll stand in the ditch to push the truck back.'

Mandy nodded, unable to speak. She felt sick at the thought of a ewe trapped under the truck. It had already been under there for ages! While the men climbed down into the ditch, Mandy carefully leaned through the window. But she couldn't quite reach.

'I'll have to open the door. I'll try not to put any weight on the truck,' she told Ken.

'Right, once you can reach the handbrake let us know, and then, on the count of three, release it and we'll all push,' Ken instructed her.

Mandy leaned into the truck without touching it but she couldn't quite reach the brake. Gingerly, she put one hand on the seat, reaching in a little bit further. Her hand closed round the lever. 'I've got it,' she shouted. 'But it won't move.'

'You have to press in the button on the end.' Mandy heard Ken's voice float up through the floor of the truck.

'Right,' she shouted back.

'OK, Mandy, one, two, three!'

Mandy pressed the button with all her strength, but nothing happened. She pressed it again as hard as her thumb could bear and then, with a snap, it gave way and the lever shifted. Mandy felt the truck jerk backwards and come to rest on the road. Quickly, she wriggled out and ran to the edge of the ditch, dreading what she was about to see.

'It's all right, Mandy,' Ken said quickly, seeing her stricken face. 'We haven't found her yet, but she's here somewhere, I'm sure.'

Mandy clambered down into the ditch and squeezed past James to the other side where the undergrowth was dense and very prickly. Further along, past where the truck had been, she spotted a pale woolly shape. 'Ken, quick, I've found her,' she cried.

Ken was beside her in a flash. 'Well done, Mandy,' he muttered, tugging away the undergrowth with his hands.

'James, fetch Dad,' Mandy called over her shoulder as she helped Ken, flinching as she accidentally grabbed hold of a stinging nettle.

'OK,' James shouted back. Mandy heard his trainers pounding along the lane towards the Land-rover.

'She must have got in a right old panic,' said Ken. 'She's halfway through the fence, almost on the other side, and . . .' he crawled under the hedge, '. . . she's caught on the wire. Do you think your dad might have some wire-cutters with him?'

Mandy had never felt so relieved as when she saw her father draw up at that moment. 'Dad,' she called. 'We need wire-cutters.'

Adam Hope jumped down and ran to the back of the Land-rover. He took out several things and hurried across the ditch to join them, handing a pair of long-handled wire-cutters to Ken. 'Here you go,' he said. 'Gosh, this young lady's got herself in a pickle, hasn't she?'

'I'm afraid her lambing has begun, Mr Hope.' Ken's voice was muffled as he struggled to cut the ewe free. 'That's got you, girl. Don't fret, we'll soon have you out of here.'

'Let me look.' Mandy's dad crawled on his hands and knees into the hedge next to Ken. 'You're right. We mustn't move her any further than is absolutely necessary,' Mandy heard him tell Ken as he examined the ewe. 'But if we could at least get her away from the hedge I can deliver her lambs here. It looks like she's struggling, and there's no time to lose.'

'Aye,' Ken muttered grimly. 'She's not due for another couple of weeks, by my reckoning.'

His words were almost drowned out by a sudden crack of thunder. Mandy hardly had time to think about fetching a waterproof jacket from the Land-rover before the heavens opened and the rain that had been threatening for the last half-hour came pouring down. Within seconds, Mandy was soaked to the skin but she didn't care about herself. She was far more worried about how much more difficult it was going to make things for the ewe. She knew from her experience with other animals that even in the perfect conditions of the Animal Ark surgery, delivering babies could be a very dangerous procedure.

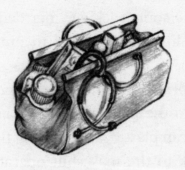

Three

Slowly and gently, Ken and Mr Hope lifted the ewe away from the fence on to the bank on the other side of the ditch. This was out of the shelter of the hedge, which meant that all of them were soon soaked through.

'She's damaged a leg, Ken,' observed Mr Hope. He frowned as he ran his hand over the sheep's heaving flank. 'But that's the least of our worries at the moment.'

'Is there anything I can do?' Mandy pleaded, desperate to do something useful.

'Would you look in the back of the Land-rover and find me some sacking?' her dad asked. 'My knees are slipping – I need to put something under them.'

Mandy sprinted over to the Land-rover. She leaped on to the bumper, reached in and found two large clean plastic sacks. Pulling them out, she rushed back to the makeshift operating theatre. 'Here, Dad,' she cried, handing them to him.

'Thanks, love,' said Mr Hope, easing one sack underneath the ewe and then shoving the other one under his knees.

'Perhaps you and James could stand on the road and keep an eye out for cars,' suggested Ken. 'This lane gets busy at lunchtime.'

'Good idea,' agreed Mr Hope. 'There's a couple of orange jackets in the Land-rover, too. Put them on; you want to be seen clearly in this weather.'

'I'll get them,' James said eagerly.

Harry Wainwright scrambled out of the ditch. 'It's better if I keep out of your way,' he said.

'Thanks, Harry,' said Mr Hope, rolling up his shirtsleeves. 'I'd sit in the Land-rover if I were you, out of the rain. Help yourself to the flask of coffee; there's no point in us all catching a chill.'

'That sounds lovely, thank you,' said Harry, setting off down the lane.

James passed him, carrying two bright orange jackets with silver stripes across the back and around the sleeves. 'This one looks smaller,' he said, handing it to Mandy. She put it on and the sleeves hung down almost to her knees. She rolled them up and pulled the collar tight. At least it stopped the rain from going down her neck. And they'd certainly be seen in these!

'I'll stay this side of the bend,' she told James, who was wrestling with his own sleeves. 'You go down the lane. That way we can see each other and let cars through one at a time if it gets busy.'

But before they could get into their positions a car came along the lane and slowed right down. The driver and his passenger craned their necks, straining to see what was going on. James walked over to him and Mandy watched as the window was wound down.

'Has there been an accident?' asked the driver in a concerned voice.

'It's a ewe in trouble,' James explained. 'But there's nothing to worry about, the vet's with her. Could you drive slowly, please, so it doesn't frighten her?'

'Oh, certainly, of course,' replied the driver, closing the window and driving on.

Mandy made a thumbs-up sign to James and walked to the bend. She glanced back to where her dad and Ken were kneeling beside the ewe, and she crossed her fingers that things were going well. Soon she saw James looking at her to see if it was safe to wave a car through and she held up her hand to halt the builder's van that was coming towards her. Its occupants were a couple of young lads, wearing paint-spattered overalls.

'What's up, love?' the driver asked cheerily, leaning out of the window. 'You broken down?' They both laughed. 'We can give you a push if you like.'

'No,' Mandy said, shaking her head. 'It's nothing like that. There's been an accident and a ewe is giving birth.'

'Oh, sorry,' said the driver. 'I didn't mean to laugh. Is it going to be all right?'

'We hope so, the vet's with her now,' Mandy told them. 'Would you drive past slowly, please, so the noise doesn't frighten her?'

'Yes, sure,' the driver promised. 'Er, is there anything we can do? Fetch anyone, or get the farmer or something?'

'Thank you for offering,' Mandy said. 'But really, everything is being done that can be done. The shepherd's here, and the vet's my dad,' she added proudly.

'Well, good luck then,' said the driver, moving slowly forward as James waved him through.

With the lane quiet, Mandy took the opportunity of creeping a little closer to the ditch to see what was happening.

'Did you say she had twins last year?' Mandy heard her dad ask.

'That's right,' Ken replied. 'She's a three-year-old now so she knows what's what. But even though her lambs weren't early last year, they were very small. She had a difficult labour.'

'Here we go, now. I think I've found the problem.' Adam Hope suddenly sounded worried. 'I should be feeling a foot or a nose but I think

I'm feeling a tail. The lamb is round the wrong way. We've got to get it out quickly, Ken, before it's starved of oxygen.'

Mandy felt her stomach lurch. It was called a breech birth, when an animal came out bottom first. She desperately hoped her dad could save the lamb. At that moment a blue estate car came along the lane and she was glad to have something to do again. Stepping forward, she halted the car and walked round to the driver's door. The young couple inside looked at her anxiously. In the back, two small boys listened wide-eyed as Mandy explained what had happened.

'Can we see the sheep?' they chorused. 'Can we?'

'No, boys,' their mother told them. 'The sheep isn't very well.'

Mandy checked with James, only to see he had quite a queue of traffic. 'Would you mind waiting a few minutes to let those cars through?' she asked the driver next to her.

'Certainly, we're in no hurry,' said the woman.

From the back of the car came the sound of a squabble as one of the boys pulled a comic from the other's hands.

'Ssh, boys, you'll scare the poorly sheep,' whispered their mum, with a wink at Mandy. The boys stopped arguing at once, and sat very still with serious expressions on their faces.

Mandy saw that James was waving at her. The family could go now. 'Look,' she said, pointing up the lane. 'Not far down there is an entrance to a field. If it's safe, you can pull in there and see a whole flock of sheep.'

With rapt expressions the two little boys stared up at Mandy.

'But don't disturb them, will you?' Mandy warned them gently. 'They're going to have their lambs very soon.'

'Don't worry, they'll behave,' the woman promised as she started the engine and drove away.

Mandy couldn't wait any longer. With one eye on the road, she edged her way along the bank. 'Dad,' she called urgently. 'What's happening?'

Ken looked round and stood up stiffly, rubbing his knees. 'It's twins again, Mandy! Your dad's just delivered the second one. The ewe's in a bad way, though. She's showing no interest in the little ones so far.'

Mandy shivered. It didn't seem fair for the ewe to go through all this and then have something else go wrong. 'What about the lambs?' she asked, anxiety making her voice tremble. 'Are they all right?'

'Aye,' Ken said, nodding. 'They're little-uns, though.' He sighed. 'I've just cleaned them up.'

'And I'm afraid the ewe's foreleg is broken,' Mr Hope told them sombrely, looking up. 'In her panic she must have caught it in the fence. I wouldn't be surprised if she's damaged the tendons too.'

'Can we move her?' asked Ken.

Adam Hope nodded, his face grim. 'I'd like to get her inside as soon as possible, now. She's in shock, and all this rain isn't helping.'

Mandy knew how serious that was – animals could die from shock, and sheep were particularly vulnerable.

'I could get the trailer,' Ken offered, 'but it would take me a while.'

'There's no time,' said Mr Hope, opening the ewe's mouth. Mandy knew he was looking at the colour of the gums to see how well the sheep's blood was circulating, and even she could see that they were very pale. Adam Hope placed his stethoscope on the ewe's neck. 'Her pulse is weak, she's cold, and her breathing is getting laboured. We'll put her in the Land-rover and I'll take her down.'

Mandy sprang into action. 'Come on, James, let's clear a space.'

'Good thinking, Mandy,' said Adam Hope. 'You two can sit in the back and look after the lambs. They're smaller than I'd like, but they're doing OK for now. Could you ask Mr Wainwright to come and give us a hand with lifting the ewe?'

'Sure,' said Mandy. She and James jogged back to the Land-rover and explained to Harry what they were going to do. He seemed only too pleased to be able to help with the injured sheep, and set off at a rather stiff-legged run back to the ditch.

Mandy dropped the tailgate of the Land-rover and she and James climbed in. She couldn't wait to see the newborn lambs but for the moment, she knew the ewe's condition was more critical. As well as feeling affection for the brave animal, Mandy knew that hill farmers like Dora and Ken simply couldn't afford to lose one of their flock.

Mandy found an old blanket to put over the ewe to keep her warm. She and James would have to snuggle the lambs under their jackets to stop them getting any colder.

'Can you take these, you two?' Ken said, appearing at the door of the Land-rover. Mandy gasped with delight as he handed her a beautiful little lamb. Its face was all white and a pair of button brown eyes gazed into hers. The lamb's tiny ears flopped down like a puppy's, instead of pointing up.

'Oh, you are gorgeous!' she whispered to the lamb.

'Here, James,' said Ken, handing him the other lamb. 'Don't go all soppy over them, you two, they're not pets,' he warned, but his eyes were twinkling.

Holding the lamb against her, Mandy watched as Mr Hope, Ken, and Harry used the sacks to lift the ewe. They carried her carefully down the road.

'I'll stay here to check the rest of the flock settles down,' puffed Ken, his gnarled fingers clenched round the edge of the sack.

'I can give you a hand wi' that,' offered Harry. 'I've got to wait for the tow-truck anyway.'

'Your mum is going to be fine,' Mandy whispered to the lamb in her arms, which had started to wriggle. 'Trust us.'

But when her dad and Ken laid the ewe on the floor of the Land-rover, Mandy noticed that her eyes were dull and glazed, and she was shivering violently under her thick fleece. Holding the lamb, Mandy dropped to her knees beside the ewe. The lamb wriggled again as it tried to reach its mother, but Mandy held it close.

'You poor thing,' she said, carefully covering the ewe with the blanket. 'Don't worry,' she soothed, gently placing her free hand on the ewe's head and stroking it. 'We'll look after you.'

The ewe's eyes rolled as Adam Hope started the engine, and Mandy hoped she had sounded more confident than she felt. Would the ewe cope with the journey to the farm? Or was it too late?

Four

Dora Janeki was in the yard when they reached Syke Farm. She gave them a quizzical look as she opened the gate to let the Land-rover through. 'What brings you here?' she asked, as Adam Hope pulled up. 'Charlie told me you had a bit of a mishap up there, but he said you were more or less finished. I expected you back a while ago.'

'It all got more complicated after Charlie left us, I'm afraid,' Mr Hope told her as he climbed out. 'We've got a ewe in the back, but she's in a bad way,' he warned, striding around to the back of the Land-rover. 'She's had twins and she's got a broken foreleg.'

'Put her in that stable nearest the house,' Dora said quickly, pointing to some outbuildings. 'It's all set for emergency treatment. I'll fetch what we need from the house.'

She hurried off as Mr Hope helped Mandy and James to climb down from the back, still holding the lambs.

'The lambs are fine, Dad.' Mandy frowned as she spoke. 'But I think they're getting very hungry.' Her lamb gave a piteous bleat, as if to agree.

'They'll have to wait a bit longer,' Adam Hope told her. 'It won't hurt them and I want to sort this young lady out first.' He leaned in to check the ewe's gums once more, then with Dora's help when she returned, gently lifted her out. 'Mandy, run and open the door for us, love, and James, bring my bag, please.'

Mandy hurried across the yard to the stable. She reached up to undo the latch on the top part of the door, being careful not to crush the lamb in her arms, then slid back the bolt and opened the lower part. Inside, the floor was covered with a thick bed of straw and there was a trough for drinking water. The old stone walls were thick enough to keep out the worst of the Yorkshire weather. It felt warm and cosy inside, in spite of the rain. Mandy's dad and Dora followed her across the yard with the sheep slung between them on the sack. They carried the ewe into the stable and laid her gently on the straw.

'I'm afraid it's not her leg I'm most worried about,' Mr Hope explained in a calm voice as he rifled through his bag, bringing out a drip and some small glass vials. 'What with the trauma of the accident and the birth, she's gone into shock.'

Dora knelt beside the ewe. 'Oh, it's you,' she said fondly. 'This one's always been a bit of a bolter, leads us all a merry old dance sometimes, trying to round her up.' She sighed. 'I hope we don't lose her,' she added in a worried voice. Mandy felt her heart wrench in sympathy.

'We're not giving up on her just yet, Dora,' said Adam Hope, optimistically. 'The first thing we need to do is give her some fluids. Then I'm going to give her a steroid injection, some antibiotics and a painkilling injection.'

'What about her milk?' asked Dora. 'Will the drugs pass through to her lambs, if she's able to suckle them, that is?' Dora bent down and examined the ewe. 'She's got plenty of milk. We feed them a high energy food supplement coming up to lambing time, so they can look after their lambs as well as possible.'

'There's nothing in these injections that will damage the lambs,' Adam Hope reassured her as he set the drip up, hooking it on to the wall. Then he filled a syringe, held it up and flicked it with his middle finger.

Dora turned to Mandy and James. 'I gather those bundles in your coats are her lambs,' she said, putting out her hands to take the lamb from James. He passed it over, giving it a quick stroke on its head as it bleated crossly. 'A tup,' Dora declared, giving it back to James. 'That means a boy,' she explained, seeing his baffled expression. She examined the lamb that Mandy held. 'And this one's a gimmer.'

'A girl?' Mandy guessed.

'That's right,' said Dora, as Mandy tucked the lamb back inside her jacket. 'Twins are always a bit weedy, compared to a single lamb,' she went on. 'But they'll do just fine. Keep them away from their mum, though, she can do without them at the moment.'

'Yes, I'll wait for a while until we see the effects of the fluids,' Adam Hope advised. 'As soon as she seems to be getting over the shock, I'll splint that leg and take out the drip.'

'No need for you to wait, Adam,' Dora said politely. 'I've splinted many a leg in my time, and will plenty more, no doubt. Time's money where vets are concerned and I don't want to take up any more of yours. Not that I'm not grateful, mind,' she added.

'Don't worry, Dora.' Mr Hope smiled. 'I shan't be putting in a bill, it's just lucky I was around. And . . .' he looked at Mandy and James's worried faces. 'I can't see my daughter leaving Syke Farm until she's sure that the ewe is recovering, so I'd have to wait anyway.'

'Thanks, Dad,' Mandy said gratefully. 'We couldn't leave yet, we've been through so much with her.' She glanced down at the ewe, who lay quietly on the straw, her flanks heaving. Her broken foreleg stuck out awkwardly to one side, and Mandy hoped that her dad's painkilling injection had started to work.

'Thank you for that, Adam,' said Dora. 'That's very good of you. So what happened in the lane, anyway? What caused all this?'

Mandy suddenly remembered Harry Wainwright and hoped he was getting on all right with the tow-truck.

'Why don't we all go inside for a cup of tea, Dora?' suggested Mr Hope. 'There's nothing more we can do for this ewe right now, and I can fill you in on the details.'

'Dad, can we stay out here?' Mandy asked. She couldn't bear not to be around to see what was happening to the ewe, good or bad.

'Well, there's really nothing to be done here, Mandy,' her dad said gently. 'And you're both wet through. Why not come in and have a drink of something?'

Mandy shook her head. 'I'm all right, Dad, honestly. I'd really rather stay here.'

'James?' Mr Hope quizzed, raising his eyebrows. 'I suppose you want to stay too?'

'Definitely,' James replied firmly.

'OK, then,' said Adam Hope. 'If that's all right with you, Dora?' he added.

Dora Janeki nodded. 'Oh, aye, I know your lass will be gentle with her.'

It was quiet in the stable when the adults had left. Mandy and James sat down in the straw with their backs against the walls. The ewe's eyes were closed but Mandy could hear the rasping of her breathing and saw her shiver occasionally. She could hardly bear the wait to see if her dad's treatment would work. She was relieved to be distracted when the lambs began fidgeting.

'Look, Mandy,' James said softly. 'He's nibbling my fingers.'

'They're probably hungry,' Mandy pointed out. 'They want their mum.' She looked across at James and saw a look of anguish suddenly appear on his face. Her eyes flew to the ewe.

'She's stopped breathing!' James exclaimed, his voice catching. 'Listen!'

Mandy listened, her heart sinking. James was

right, the harsh raspy noise had stopped and the
ewe was silent. Carefully she passed her lamb to
James and he held it on his lap. Mandy crawled
through the straw and knelt beside the ewe.
Leaning forward, she put her hand in front of the
ewe's mouth. She couldn't feel anything. Mandy
couldn't remember ever feeling so miserable.
Sitting back on her heels she watched the sheep
through stinging eyes. And as she watched, she
realised that the animal's chest *was* rising and
falling. She *was* breathing.

'James!' Mandy whispered. 'She *is* breathing, but
she's breathing normally now, that's why we
couldn't hear her.' She reached out and carefully
lifted one side of the ewe's mouth. 'Look, her
gums are pink and . . .' Mandy pressed her finger
gently on the gum and watched as it became pale
then pink again as the blood rushed back almost
immediately. 'See that? That's called the capillary
refill time. It means that her circulation has
improved, almost back to normal, I think.'

The ewe jerked her head away from Mandy's
hand as if she didn't like her lip being pulled.
'That's a good sign,' Mandy said with a laugh. 'You

know what? I think she's going to be all right.'

As if to confirm this, the ewe opened her eyes, lifted her head and gave a soft bleating call.

'Wow,' said James, jumping as both lambs tried to squirm away to join their mother.

'I hope she'll be well enough to feed them soon,' Mandy said.

'Your dad will have to splint her leg first,' James cautioned.

'That won't take him long,' Mandy assured him, grabbing her lamb and tucking it inside her coat.

'Well, how are we doing?' Mr Hope's voice came from the door. 'Any improvement?'

'She's much better, Dad,' Mandy told him happily. 'She's breathing normally, her gums are pink and the capillary refill time is good.'

'You've got a vet in the making there,' Dora remarked. 'Starting her young, are you?' She looked down at Mandy who grinned back. She loved helping her parents at Animal Ark, and was determined to be a vet when she was older.

'I can't keep her away from animals, Dora,' Mandy's dad sighed. 'She'll be telling her old dad what to do soon.'

'Da-ad!' Mandy groaned, wrinkling her nose. 'As if.'

'You're absolutely right here, though,' Adam Hope went on, kneeling down to examine the ewe. 'She's recovering well. Let's do her leg and take out her drip and then I really must get on, I've got a couple of calls to make.'

The ewe gave a disgruntled bleat and gave Adam Hope a look of indignation as he gently took hold of her leg.

'I've delivered her lambs, saved her life and brought her here in the Land-rover, and she's still cross with me!' Mr Hope joked. 'There's no pleasing sheep!'

'That's true,' Dora agreed. From out of her pocket she took a short piece of plastic piping that had been cut lengthways in two. Mandy felt a bit surprised.

Dora noticed her expression. 'It's waste pipe,' she explained. 'I used to use a ruler but this works much better. You can pad it out with lots of cotton wool and it's much more comfortable for the sheep.' She passed the two padded sections to Mr Hope and he placed them round the ewe's leg. Mandy could see it was a perfect solution.

'It works just as well as anything I'd use,' Adam Hope agreed. 'I'll tape it up fairly firmly today,' he said, pulling a length of sticking plaster from the roll and winding it around the splint. The ewe seemed happy to lie still, watching him with curious yellow eyes as he gently removed the drip. 'There, she's done.' He added, 'She's still a bit weak to take her lambs, though. Do you have some bottles for them, Dora?'

'Oh, aye,' said Dora. 'I'll get Charlie to give me a hand feeding them as soon as he gets back.'

'Is it OK to put the lambs with their mum now?' Mandy asked. 'Even if they can't feed?'

'Sure,' said Adam Hope.

Mandy and James put them down in the straw and watched in delight as they took their first wobbly but determined steps towards their mother. The ewe muttered at them while they pressed their tiny bodies against her thick woolly fleece. The ewe lay on her side with her splinted leg stuck straight out in front, her eyes warm with pride in her lambs.

'What will you call them?' Mandy asked Dora, as they watched the scene.

Dora snorted and shook her head. 'I don't name them, Mandy,' she said. 'They'll be numbers in the record book.'

'But what's the ewe's name?' Mandy persisted. 'She's got a name, hasn't she?'

'I'd soon run out of ideas if I gave all the flock names,' Dora tutted, picking up the box of bandages. 'But I suppose you can name them, if you want to.'

'Yes, please,' said Mandy, then she hesitated. 'I think I'll call the ewe Rebecca, and the lambs . . .' She put her hands on her hips and studied the two little creatures. 'You can be Rudy,' she told the tup lamb. 'And your sister can be Rhonda. What do you think, James?'

'Great!' he said.

'Very fancy,' Dora said drily. 'You'll have the rest of the flock jealous. Not the same being called SF35, is it?'

'All the Rrrrrrrrrrs,' said Adam Hope, exaggerating the sound of the letter. 'Now, Dora, is there anything else these two can do for you before we go?'

'James, would you like to get an armful of hay from the barn?' Dora asked. 'I'll get her a bowl of sugar beet nuts, and put fresh water in the trough for her. She won't be able to walk on that leg for a couple of days, so we'll need to make sure she can reach her food easily.'

When James got back to the stable with a great sheaf of hay, Mandy spread it on the ground in front of Rebecca. She placed the bowl of food Dora gave her near to Rebecca's head, gave her a quick pat and followed the others out of the stable. Behind her, she could hear Rebecca nosing the sugar beet nuts. Mandy felt a surge of relief – if the ewe was feeling hungry, that was a sign that she was definitely on the mend.

'You can leave the top door open,' Dora told them when they were all out in the yard. 'I'll keep a check on her, and close it later.' She walked with them to the Land-rover. 'I'm obliged to all of you,' she said. 'For your time, and help and that.'

'Think nothing of it, Dora,' said Mr Hope. 'Glad we could make ourselves useful.'

Mandy and James waved to Dora as she let them out of the gate. Then Mandy sat back in the seat, suddenly feeling worn out. Something dug into her leg, and she leaned down to investigate.

'Guess what I've just found?' she said, laughing. 'Our picnic! Here you are, James.' She unpacked the sandwiches and handed them round. 'I don't know about you, but I'm starving!'

Mandy woke the next morning with butterflies of excitement in her stomach. Her first thoughts were of Rebecca, Rudy and Rhonda. How had the lambs enjoyed their first night in the world? she wondered. Springing out of bed she opened the curtains and leaned out of the window. The sun was warm and a cockerel crowed somewhere in the village. The smell of coffee drifted up the stairs. Mandy pulled on trousers and a T-shirt and raced downstairs into the kitchen.

'Morning, love,' her dad greeted her as he sliced a large brown loaf. 'Want some toast?'

'Just one slice, please,' Mandy said. She sat down at the scrubbed pine table and poured herself a glass of apple juice. 'I wonder how Rebecca and her lambs are this morning?'

'If I had to hazard a guess,' Mr Hope said, smiling, and putting a plate of toast on the table, 'I'd say they were just fine.'

'Rebecca couldn't, well, have a relapse, could she?' Mandy asked, pausing as she buttered the toast. She knew that animals sometimes appeared to be getting better, then suddenly took a turn for the worse.

'I'd be very surprised,' her dad replied. 'Hill sheep are incredibly hardy.' He leaned against the sink, eating a slice of toast. 'I remember one winter when some hill sheep were buried under six feet of snow. One of them had been buried for eight days by the time they got her out. There was nothing wrong with her apart from feeling a bit cold and hungry!'

'Now *that* is hardy,' said Mandy's mum from the doorway. Emily Hope had been told the whole story about the Syke Farm sheep the night before. 'But what I want to know,' she said, joining them at the table, 'is what made you give them those names? I mean Rudy and Rhonda are fine for lambs but Rebecca, well, it's not very,' she searched for a word, 'very sheepy!' she finished with a laugh.

'I think it's *very* sheepy,' Mandy insisted, joining in the laughter. 'Anyway, she looks like a Rebecca, doesn't she, Dad?'

'Er, I don't think I'll get drawn in on that one, Mandy,' said Mr Hope. 'But I'll probably call at Syke Farm this morning, so I can judge for myself. Do you and James want to come?'

'Yes, please, Dad,' Mandy said, jumping up from the table. 'I'll just ring James to tell him.'

James was really keen. 'I'll wait at the end of

the drive. It will be brilliant to see how the three Rs are doing!'

'Take your wellies, Mandy,' advised Mrs Hope, gathering up the empty plates. 'It will be very muddy after all that rain yesterday.'

'Thanks, Mum,' Mandy said, picking up her boots from beside the back door. 'I'll put them in the Land-rover.'

'And don't be too late back,' her mother added, smiling as Mandy dropped a kiss on her cheek. 'Summer term starts tomorrow, don't forget.'

'As if I could!' Mandy joked. She enjoyed school but she preferred being with animals. And particularly on such a special morning as this, with Rebecca and Rudy and Rhonda to visit.

Five

Mandy and her dad stopped on the way to Syke Farm to pick up James, who was waiting at the end of his drive as he promised. Mandy was relieved to see he was wearing wellies, too. She moved over so he could sit next to her on the front seat.

'Thanks, Mr Hope,' said James, shutting the door. 'I can't wait to see Rebecca and the lambs.'

'Me too,' Mandy agreed.

Soon the familiar sight of the farm came into view at the end of the valley. The moor that loomed behind the grey stone buildings looked warm and welcoming in the sun today, but Mandy knew that in the winter it could seem a very barren and bleak place.

'Look, there's Dora,' said James, pointing across one of the nearby fields as he got out to open the gate.

Dora looked as if she was busy mending a fence, but she had heard them arrive and gave them a thumbs-up with both hands. Mandy guessed that meant Rebecca, Rudy and Rhonda were all right. As soon as her dad pulled up in the yard, she scrambled out of the Land-rover with James close behind her. She felt a shiver of nervous excitement when she opened the door of the stable and stepped inside.

Rudy and Rhonda immediately trotted towards her, nuzzling up against her legs and nibbling at her shoelaces. 'Hello, you two!' Mandy exclaimed, crouching down to rub their soft bodies. She felt a thrill of delight that they seemed to recognise her. Rebecca raised her head from the straw and gazed at Mandy with bright eyes.

'Hello, old girl,' said Mr Hope, kneeling down

beside the ewe and taking his stethoscope from his bag. 'That all sounds good,' he told Mandy, who went over to kneel beside him. 'Her heart's fine now, but it's a bit soon to put her back with the flock. We'll give her a few days inside. But she doesn't want to be lying around for too long; that won't do her any good at all. Grazing animals like sheep, cows and horses are designed to spend most of their time on their feet, moving around. They can't digest their food properly if they lie down. I would like to get Rebecca up today, even if it's just for a few minutes.'

'We can help,' Mandy offered.

'Well, James, could you keep the lambs out of the way?' Mandy's dad suggested. 'Then I'll lift Rebecca up to a standing position. Mandy, you could make sure her splinted leg doesn't get caught under her.'

Mandy shuffled closer to Rebecca's shoulder and gently scratched the ewe's woolly head, trying to reassure her. Rebecca's eyes were very wide with all this attention, and she was looking a bit alarmed.

'One, two, three, now!' said Adam Hope,

placing one hand round Rebecca's chest and the other under her tail.

With Mandy supporting her broken leg, he heaved the sheep on to her feet. But as soon as he let go, her legs started to buckle, and she bleated in protest.

'Keep holding her up until she steadies herself,' Adam Hope advised.

Mandy quickly changed position. 'Good girl, Rebecca,' she whispered, kneeling with her arms around Rebecca's neck, supporting her and breathing in her distinctive sheepy smell. The ewe wobbled and stood still, muttering darkly at them all.

Mandy grinned across the table at James, who returned her smile over his armful of lambs.

'See if you can get her to take a few steps, Mandy,' said Mr Hope, standing back. 'I'd like to see her put some weight on that leg.'

Mandy encouraged the sheep to walk forwards but Rebecca wouldn't budge. 'Maybe if we put Rudy and Rhonda down a little way away, she might move towards them,' she suggested.

'OK,' said her dad. He nodded to James. 'Don't

let them run at her, though,' he warned.

James put the lambs down and gently restrained them.

Rebecca was standing more steadily now. 'Go on,' Mandy urged, as the ewe tentatively touched her splinted leg to the ground. 'You can do it.'

'Step away, Mandy,' Adam Hope said softly.

Mandy backed away until she felt the wall behind her. Rebecca glanced at Mandy, and then at her lambs. Taking a deep breath, she hopped bravely towards them, hardly putting her splinted leg to the ground, but managing to stay upright on her three good legs.

'Let her lambs go, James,' Adam Hope told him.

As soon as James released his gentle hold on the lambs, they scurried over to their mum, mouths reaching underneath her, their tails wiggling with pleasure. Rebecca rocked a bit, then regained her balance and stood as still as a rock while her lambs suckled.

Mandy felt a lump in her throat at the ewe's bravery and she swallowed hard. 'And she's even feeding them now!' she said in delight.

'How long will the splint have to stay on?' asked James.

'About six to eight weeks, but she's tough so she should heal pretty quickly,' Mr Hope replied, closing his vet bag and making for the door. 'Let's take a quick look in the lambing fields before we go. Grab your wellies from the Land-rover, Mandy, and I'll meet you down there.'

Mandy was glad she'd brought her boots, as the grass in the field was muddy and churned up after all the rain. There were several more lambs trotting about on unsteady legs, but Ken and Charlie were nowhere to be seen.

'I expect they're resting back at the farm,' Adam Hope said. 'Sheep seem to choose the middle of the night to give birth, so lambing is a hard time for sheep farmers. Luckily, everything seems to be absolutely fine here, in spite of the interrupted nights.' He grinned. 'Whereas alpacas always give birth around mid-morning, which makes the sheep farmers really jealous.'

'Alpacas?' echoed James. 'Here? But they're like llamas, aren't they? I thought they came from Peru.'

'They do, James. But they're being bred here too,' explained Adam Hope. 'There's quite a big alpaca farm in Cumbria, where a friend of mine is a vet.'

Mandy smiled to herself as her boots sluiced through the mud. Her dad was full of surprises!

Later that day Mandy was in her bedroom, getting her things ready for school the next day. Her mother came in with her clean uniform.

'Dad tells me that Rebecca is doing fine,' said Emily Hope, sitting on the bed and watching Mandy pack her school bag. 'And that Rudy and Rhonda are filling out already.'

'They're great,' Mandy agreed. 'You'd never know they'd been born early, in the middle of a lane!'

'Lambing must be well underway now at Syke Farm,' Mrs Hope went on, running her hand through her red hair. 'It's a really busy time for them, they'll miss you and James helping out.'

Mandy grinned and pushed her shoulder-length blonde hair behind her ears. 'It was great being up there in the holidays,' she admitted. 'And I'll miss Rebecca and the lambs.'

'I need to see Dora about some wool for Gran, actually,' Mrs Hope told her. 'If you like, you and James can come with me. How about tomorrow after school?'

'Yes, please,' Mandy said enthusiastically. She was dying to find out if Rebecca was able to walk on her splinted leg yet; Mandy also had to admit that she didn't want Rudy and Rhonda to forget who she was!

The next day Mandy and James cycled back to Animal Ark as fast as they could and quickly changed out of their school clothes.

'What does Gran want the wool for?' Mandy quizzed her mum as they drove up to Syke Farm.

'It's just an idea I had,' explained Emily Hope. 'Gran's thinking about setting up a knitting circle and I wondered whether Dora's sheep could provide the wool.'

'That would be good for Dora as well, wouldn't it?' said James.

'Yes, although I don't think Gran will be able to use *all* the wool she produces!' Emily Hope said with a smile. 'Years ago, knitting was a big cottage industry in the Dales, and sheep farmers had to work hard to keep up with local demand. But nowadays nearly all the wool goes to big textile companies in the city,' she finished as they drove through the open gate.

Mandy had the door open almost before Mrs Hope had turned off the engine. 'How's Rebecca?' she called out to Dora who was standing by the stable door.

'And Rudy and Rhonda?' added James, scrambling out of the Land-rover behind Mandy.

'See for yourselves,' Dora said as they joined her. 'She won't run a race yet, but she's not doing bad.'

Mandy opened the stable door and went in. 'Come and meet them, Mum,' she called over her shoulder. 'Aren't they gorgeous?'

'They certainly know you,' Emily Hope remarked, as first the lambs and then Rebecca came up to Mandy, nudging her legs with their hard little heads. To Mandy's delight, Rebecca was actually putting some weight on her injured foreleg now, although her head nodded with the effort of limping just a few steps.

'Here, give Rebecca a couple of these,' said Dora, taking some sugar beet nuts from her pocket and passing them to Mandy. 'You might like to go up to the lambing field, as well. Charlie and me were up all night, and we haven't lost a single lamb yet!' she announced, touching the stable door. 'Touch wood!'

Mandy looked at her mother. 'Have we got time, Mum?'

'Of course,' answered Emily Hope. 'It will give me a chance to have a chat with Dora.'

Mandy and James made their way up to the lambing field and climbed on to the gate. 'Look, James!' Mandy exclaimed. 'Almost every ewe has got a lamb with her now. Isn't that amazing?'

'There's Charlie,' said James, pointing to the far corner of the field. 'What's he holding? It looks too small to be a lamb.'

Mandy hopped over the gate into the field and they jogged across the grass. When they reached Charlie, Mandy was shocked to see that it was indeed a lamb, but much smaller than all the others. Charlie gave a curt nod in their direction, but didn't stop what he was doing. He held the lamb in one arm, and with his other hand he was repeatedly bending the little lamb's forefeet up and down, up and down. It reminded Mandy of the ankle-flexing exercises her dad did before he went for a run.

'This one's a proper weakling,' said Charlie. 'He's only just been born.'

'What's wrong with him?' asked James, stumbling forward slightly as a sheep barged into the back of his legs. 'Hey, shoo!' he protested, giving the ewe a gentle push away.

'He's got shortened tendons in his front legs,' Charlie explained. 'It happens sometimes. Look, his feet are bent right back under him, where the tendons are too tight. They'll get better in their own time, but for the moment he can't walk.'

'But surely his mother will look after him, won't she?' Mandy asked, alarmed.

'No, she's abandoned him,' Charlie said bluntly. 'His mother's a shearling, which means she's two years old, young and silly she is. This little fellow is one of twins; took me hours to make her suckle the first one. She kept running away, as if she was frightened of her own lamb!' He looked down at the fuzzy bundle in his arms. 'She didn't want to know this one at all. He couldn't keep up with her anyway, not being able to walk.'

Mandy's eyes stung as she stroked the lamb's tiny head. 'What's going to happen to him then?' she asked quietly.

'He's going to have to learn to walk,' Charlie explained, tiredly. 'I can't see his mum wanting him, that's for sure.' Charlie was younger than Mandy's dad, but today Mandy thought he looked as old as Ken and Dora. She could see that he was exhausted and wondered if there was anything she and James could do to help.

'He'll have to be fed with goat's milk, and we'll have to make sure he gets the colostrum he needs,' Charlie went on. 'Colostrum contains all the goodness he'd normally get from his mother's milk,' he added, trying to stifle a yawn. 'Young animals need that when they're born, it gives them protection from bugs and makes them strong.'

Mandy thought hard, twisting a piece of the lamb's soft fleece between her fingers. 'I've got it,' she announced so suddenly that the little lamb blinked with surprise. 'Rebecca can't get about very much while she's got her leg in a splint. Maybe we could try the lamb with her?' Mandy felt her enthusiasm bubbling to the surface. 'She's a wonderful mum to her own lambs and I'm sure she'd make a brilliant foster mum. What do you think?'

'I'm not sure it would work,' Charlie said simply, bringing her down to earth with a bump. 'It's unlikely she'd take on another lamb while she's got two of her own. I'm sorry.'

'What a shame,' Mandy said, feeling disheartened that her suggestion had been so easily dismissed. 'But couldn't we try?' she begged. 'Surely it's worth a chance?'

Charlie shook his head. 'Sheep can be very fussy animals. Especially that ewe! You might be wasting your time.'

'But we might not,' James pointed out. 'Rebecca knows us now. I mean, she's not frightened of us or anything.'

Charlie pushed back his cap and scratched his head, then he pulled the peak down on his forehead and frowned at the lamb.

Mandy could sense that he was weakening.

'Please, Charlie, we've nothing to lose,' she pleaded softly.

'And everything to gain,' added James.

'Well, there is a way it's been known to work, or so I've been told,' Charlie said in a resigned voice. 'But we don't have the equipment.'

Mandy felt her heart give a leap. 'Tell us how, anyway,' she begged.

'You'd need to take her lambs out, so she can't see them and then fix . . .' He looked quizzically at Mandy.

'Rebecca,' Mandy reminded him.

'Yes, Rebecca,' Charlie repeated. 'Then you'd fix Rebecca's head in a stock so she couldn't move or see the new lamb, and then you'd put him to her. But like I say, we don't have a stock.'

'Right, but if we did all that, what then?' Mandy demanded. She was already forming a plan in her head.

'Then, you'd cross your fingers and hope for the best,' Charlie said with a grin as he handed over the lamb. 'Here, we'll have to take him back to the farm anyway to feed by hand, so you may as well ask Dora what she thinks of your idea.'

Tenderly, Mandy took the tiny creature from Charlie. 'Oh James,' she said in a worried voice, as they hurried back across the field. 'There's nothing of him, he feels like a rag doll. We've *got* to make it work.'

'But he won't even be able to stand up,' James reminded her, watching the lamb's front legs dangle uselessly from Mandy's arms. Charlie was right, the soft front hooves were bent right back against the fetlock joint.

'But we have to try.' Mandy kissed the top of the lamb's head. 'I couldn't put Rebecca in a stock, though. She's been through enough as it is.'

'Good,' said James with a sigh of relief. 'I didn't fancy that either. What do you think we should do instead?'

Mandy gave him a sideways glance. 'You can hold Rebecca's head, to stop her turning round,' she said firmly.

'Oh, thanks!' James spluttered, stopping in his tracks. 'So I've got to be a human stock?'

'That's it exactly,' Mandy replied. She turned to look back at him. 'Come on James, I'm sure Rebecca won't mind.'

'Hmm,' James muttered, running to catch up with her. 'I'm not so sure about that. These sheep are pretty strong, you know.'

'Trust me, James,' Mandy said, grinning at him over the lamb's head.

When they reached the stable, Mandy's mum and Dora were talking just inside the door.

'That's a tiddler, without a doubt,' said Dora, raising her eyebrows when Mandy showed her the lamb from the field. 'He could stand all four legs on a postage stamp. What's Charlie sent him up for?'

'Well,' Mandy began to explain. 'He's got a problem with his feet, and his mother doesn't want him, and he's very hungry, and,' she faltered, 'and I told Charlie that Rebecca would feed him,' she finished, her heart sinking at the look of utter disbelief on Dora's face.

'And Charlie agreed to it?' asked Dora. 'The man must be going mad!'

'Well, he didn't exactly agree to it,' Mandy admitted. 'I sort of persuaded him to let me try.'

'Mandy,' Emily Hope said reproachfully, 'you

mustn't interfere, you know. Charlie has been a shepherd for almost all his life, so it's worth listening to him.'

'But we can try, can't we?' Mandy said, feeling tears well in her eyes and determinedly blinking them away. 'Can't we, Dora?'

Dora laughed softly, shaking her head. 'A ewe that's got her own lambs is unlikely to let another lamb go anywhere near her. Besides, she won't have enough milk for three.'

'That's not a problem,' James put in. 'A friend of ours has got a goat farm. I'm sure she'd give us some milk for him, so we can help feed him. It would just be nice to know that this lamb has a foster mother, so he doesn't feel abandoned.'

'Let me see his feet,' said Mrs Hope. 'It looks like he's got weak tendons.'

'That's it, that's what Charlie said,' Mandy told her. 'He can't stand up or walk, but they will get better on their own, apparently. That's another reason why Rebecca can help, because she won't be able to run away from him like his mother has.'

'Now there is something you could do to help him with his tendons,' said Emily Hope. 'You could try some physiotherapy on him. But you must let Dora decide what to do as far as feeding him is concerned.'

'Go on then,' Dora relented. 'You can try to put him with this ewe here, if you want. But I still think you're wasting your time,' she warned.

'Thank you, Dora,' Mandy said, beaming. 'Come on, James. And Dora, please would you take Rudy and Rhonda out?'

'I get it,' Dora said, knowingly. 'Charlie told you about a stock, did he?' Obligingly she bent down and picked up the lambs, tucked one under each arm, and went outside the stable. 'Come on, let's see this miracle then,' she said with a frown, but her voice was kind. Emily Hope stood beside her, stroking Rudy's woolly head as she watched curiously.

Mandy closed the bottom half of the door then said in a calm voice, 'James, would you hold the lamb for a moment, while I speak to Rebecca?' She handed James the lamb and went over to where Rebecca stood, warily watching the people in the doorway. Mandy knelt down, put her arms around Rebecca's neck and spoke softly in her

ear. She told her about the tiny lamb that had
been abandoned because of its poorly feet, and
how he needed looking after. When she had
finished, she took the lamb from James, saying
quietly, 'Just hold Rebecca's head, please, James.'

James crouched down in front of the ewe.
Gently he put his hands behind her ears and
cupped her head in his hands. Rebecca looked
back at him with unblinking yellow eyes. He

nodded to Mandy. She squatted down beside Rebecca and put her hand on the sheep's back. Rebecca gave a little shudder then relaxed under Mandy's touch.

Mandy moved the lamb nearer and nearer to the ewe until its eager mouth was almost touching Rebecca's udder. In spite of his crooked front legs, he was certainly hungry, with all the instincts of a newborn animal. Mandy moved the lamb forward the last bit and felt him connect with the ewe. The lamb gave a muffled bleat of delight. Mandy looked at James and smiled at their achievement.

Suddenly, without warning Mandy felt herself flying backwards, the lamb landing on top of her. Rebecca had wrenched herself out of James's hands and was prancing wildly round the pen on her three good legs, with her splinted leg dragging through the straw. James was sprawled on his back, a look of astonishment on his face.

At last Rebecca stood still. She fixed Mandy with a stare that seemed to say, 'I didn't say it would be easy.'

'Told you so,' said Dora from the doorway, her voice full of amusement. 'You'd best fetch that lamb out from there.'

'One more try, please,' Mandy said, still determined. 'She's just testing me. Can you take her head again, James?'

'OK,' said James as he got to his knees, brushing the straw from his clothes and pushing his glasses back up his nose. Rebecca eyed him suspiciously as James took hold of her again.

Mandy took a deep breath. 'Right, Rebecca,' she said gently. 'Now can we do it properly, please?' And without hesitation, she put the lamb to the ewe. As eagerly as before, the lamb began to suck. Mandy waited for Rebecca to jump away again, but she didn't. She just stood, her three good legs braced in the straw, as the little lamb drank and drank. Mandy felt a rush of delight. Her plan had worked. It really had worked!

When the lamb had finished, and Mandy could feel that his tummy was full, she handed him to James and gave Rebecca the biggest hug she could manage. 'You're a star, Rebecca,' she told the bemused ewe, who looked round as if to ask what on earth was going on. 'An absolute star.'

Standing up, Mandy took the lamb from James and walked over to the door.

'Well, bless my soul, Mandy Hope,' Dora said admiringly. 'If I had a hat on I'd eat it!'

'Well done, Mandy and James,' enthused Mrs Hope. 'You did a great job.'

Mandy looked down at the lamb and stroked his soft head. 'Well, who could resist such a sweet little lamb?' she joked. 'By the way his name's Fleet. Because when we get him better he'll the most fleet-footed lamb in the flock.'

Dora pretended to look aghast. 'Such fancy names my sheep are getting nowadays,' she tutted. 'Fleet! Whatever next?'

Mrs Hope was examining Fleet's crooked legs. 'He needs regular work on his feet,' she told them. 'Gentle massage to strengthen the tendons, as well as lots of flexing to stretch them. And support his body and make him try to stand up, gradually letting him take a bit more weight each day.'

Dora nodded. 'Aye, I'll do what I can. But with

all my sheep lambing, this little chap couldn't have picked a worse time for needing special care!'

'We can come after school,' Mandy offered, as James nodded agreement.

'Every day,' he added.

'And don't forget he'll need an extra feed with that goat's milk you were telling me about,' Dora reminded them. 'That ewe won't have enough milk for three. I've a drop in the freezer I can give him in the morning, but that's it.'

'No problem. We can call in and get some more from Lydia,' Mandy suggested. 'On our way over tomorrow.'

'That's settled then,' said Mrs Hope. 'But remember to make time for any homework you might get,' she added with a smile. 'OK, Dora, let's put all three lambs back with Rebecca.'

Mandy laid the sleepy lamb on the straw and watched carefully as Rudy and Rhonda immediately came over to investigate. They nuzzled Fleet cautiously, as if they knew he wasn't quite as strong as they were. Mandy beamed. All four of these sheep had had a tough time recently, but it looked as if they would be able to help each other through. Mandy just had to straighten Fleet's crooked forelegs, and life at Syke Farm would be perfect!

Mrs Hope drove them home in time for Mandy to help at evening surgery. She could hardly wait to tell her dad the latest news about Rebecca. But her parents were very busy, and Mandy had to concentrate on helping Jean Knox in reception and assisting her dad in the treatment room. Only when they'd finished and she was clearing up, was she able to tell her dad all about her afternoon at Syke Farm.

'That's an unusual relationship, Mandy,' remarked Mr Hope, when he'd heard about Rebecca and Fleet. 'I bet Dora was surprised.'

'She was amazed,' Mandy grinned, then turned as Jean looked round the door.

'Can you squeeze in one more patient?' she asked. 'This man's car is being repaired apparently and he's had to walk here. He's a bit puffed and I don't like to send him away.'

'Show him in, Jean,' said Adam Hope, and then exclaimed, 'Mr Wainwright!' as the old man came in. 'What a surprise, what can we do for you?'

'I'm sorry to keep you late but I'm not as young as I used to be and I can't walk so fast. Mind you, I don't live far away, just over at Monkton Spinney,' he explained, putting a carrying box on the table. 'It's just that my regular vet's on holiday, and I saw how great you were with that poor old sheep, so I wondered if you'd consider treating my birds?'

'Have they all come home?' Mandy asked eagerly.

'Not all of them, I'm afraid,' Harry answered sadly, opening the box. 'Just six so far. This one came home today with a damaged claw. It looks infected to me.'

'Mmn, nasty,' said Adam Hope as he examined the pigeon. 'But she's in good health otherwise. I'll clean the wound and give you some antibiotic powder. Sprinkle a little on every day.'

'That's very kind of you,' said Harry, gently smoothing the bird's wings. 'Now tell me, how are the sheep and her lambs?'

'They're doing fine,' Mandy said warmly. 'Rebecca's walking on her leg now, and Rudy and Rhonda are putting on weight.'

'I'm very glad to hear it,' said Harry. 'At least someone's doing well after all this.'

'Will your birds find their way home soon?' asked Adam Hope.

'I reckon they will eventually,' Harry replied. 'They know where they're well off. The young ones would have been so excited they'd probably have overshot the loft and be miles away by now. I'll have to wait for them to work out where they are, and come back. It's Super Sam I'm worried about, really.'

'Super Sam?' Mandy echoed, puzzled.

'He's my champion, the best racing pigeon in the world,' Harry explained proudly, his eyes lighting up. 'And he's a beauty – jet black with a white patch shaped like an "S" above his right eye.'

'Surely if he's experienced, he'll find his way home, won't he?' Mandy asked.

'He should,' Harry agreed. 'But there's been a goshawk circling over Piper's Wood recently, not far from where I had that accident. Birds of prey can attack pigeons,' he said, shaking his head sadly. 'Try as I might, I can't help feeling something bad has happened to Super Sam.'

Six

As Mandy and James cycled to Lydia Fawcett's farm to collect some goats' milk the next day, they discussed Harry's missing pigeons.

'I didn't realise that Harry had lost his *champion* bird,' James said thoughtfully. 'He must be really upset about it.'

'He was,' Mandy told him. 'He tried to hide it though.'

They cycled past Beacon House and the gates of Upper Welford Hall, where Sam Western lived. Mandy signalled to turn left then stood up and pedalled hard to get a good start up the unmade road that led to High Cross Farm. She was hot and out of breath when they reached the farm at the top of the hill but seeing Houdini, her favourite goat, trotting restlessly in his field, she didn't stop to rest.

'Houdini!' Mandy jumped off her bike and called him anxiously. 'What's up, boy?' She put her hand through the fence and stroked his sleek black coat. There was an anxious look in his intelligent green eyes. Mandy stroked him gently until he relaxed and began to nibble at the grass again.

'Let's go and find Lydia,' suggested James. 'It's not like Houdini to be spooked like this. I wonder what's up?'

Mandy picked up her bike and they crossed the small courtyard to the old stone house. She pushed the red front door but it resisted firmly. 'It's locked!' she announced, surprised. 'Lydia never locks her door, does she?' She rapped on the door with her knuckles. 'Run and look in the barn, James.' Mandy bit her lip, and looked at her watch. 'Though it's too early for evening milking.'

She called out, 'Lydia, it's us, Mandy and James.'

Mandy stepped back and studied the house. Out of the corner of her eye she detected a movement at the downstairs window.

'She's not in the barn,' James reported as he jogged back across the yard, spreading his hands wide. 'Where can she be?'

'It's OK, James,' Mandy told him softly. 'I think she's in the house, listen.'

Through the door came a scraping sound, followed by the clank of bolts drawn from their boltholes. Mandy and James exchanged puzzled glances. What was going on? Finally they heard the clink of a key turning in a lock.

'Lydia?' Mandy exclaimed as the door opened a crack.

'Thank goodness.' Lydia poked her head out of the doorway, her glance sweeping round the yard. 'Quick, get inside before they come back.' She pulled Mandy and James into the house and slammed the door shut behind them.

'Who?' Mandy asked, thoroughly confused. This wasn't like Lydia at all.

'The prowlers, of course!' Lydia hissed. 'They've

been casing the joint for the last couple of days now!'

Mandy's mouth dropped open in amazement. 'Casing the joint?' she asked. 'As in, checking it out for a burglary?'

'Exactly,' Lydia said.

'But who *are* they?' James asked, bewildered. 'And what are they after?'

'That's what I'd like to know, James.' Lydia folded her arms. 'I've seen two of them through my spyglass,' she said, indicating a small telescope on the windowsill. 'Looking around the perimeter fence, they were. There could be a whole gang of them for all I know, waiting out there to get me.'

'Do you really think they could be burglars?' James asked her.

Mandy exchanged glances with James. They both knew that Lydia didn't really have anything worth stealing, apart from her beautiful goats. And much as Mandy loved them, she couldn't imagine anyone being foolish enough to try kidnapping the strong-willed animals!

'Maybe they are, James,' said Lydia. 'That's why I locked the door. If they come back again, I shall call the police. Though I really don't want to bother them in case I'm wrong. I mean, what have *I* got that a burglar could possibly want?'

'Nothing I can think of, apart from the goats,' Mandy agreed diplomatically. 'What did they look like, the two you saw? Can you describe them?'

'I can indeed,' Lydia said confidently. 'They're rough-looking, in fact, they look positively dangerous, and the car is a big old green estate car, big enough to carry off all my worldly goods, I should imagine.'

'You've seen their car?' asked James, surprised.

'Oh, yes,' Lydia retorted. 'And this morning the one with the long hair came banging on the door while I was in the milking shed. I stayed put till he went away.'

'They don't sound as if they were behaving much like burglars,' Mandy said. She was baffled but worried, too. Lydia was very isolated up here; her nearest neighbour was Sam Western in Upper Welford Hall and Mandy guessed that he wouldn't be much help. She knew for a fact that he hated Lydia's goats. Customers sometimes came up to buy milk or cheese but they were not very regular visitors. In fact, not many people visited Lydia at all, which made the presence of two strange men even more suspicious. 'Something has upset Houdini as well,' Mandy told Lydia. 'He seemed agitated.'

James gasped. 'Lydia, you don't think they want to kidnap Houdini, do you?'

Lydia laughed for the first time since they'd arrived. 'They'll have their work cut out for them if they do,' she said. Mandy silently agreed with her. Then a worried look crossed Lydia's face. 'But my other goats are much more docile than Houdini. Perhaps I should lock the barn at night, at least while they're hanging around. But you haven't come here just to see me,' Lydia went on, sounding more like her normal self. 'What can I do for you?'

'We're looking after a newborn lamb up at Syke Farm,' Mandy explained. 'His name's Fleet.'

'And you need some goat's milk for him,' Lydia interrupted. 'Of course, I've a fresh batch here, take as much as you want.'

'We'll just take one small carton, please,' Mandy said.

James opened his mouth to speak but Mandy gave him a look and he closed it again.

As soon as they were on their way again and out of earshot James stopped his bike. 'That won't be nearly enough milk,' he accused Mandy. 'Why didn't you take a larger carton?'

'Because I'm worried about Lydia and these men watching the place,' Mandy explained. 'This gives us a good excuse to call in every day and keep an eye on her.'

'Right,' James agreed, nodding slowly. 'Good thinking. But will it cut down on the time we can spend on Fleet's physiotherapy?'

'A bit, but we'll just have to work harder with him while we're there!' Mandy declared, whooping as she freewheeled down the road that led to Syke Farm.

They parked their bikes in the yard and James went into the house to collect the feeding bottle that Dora had promised to leave for them.

Mandy opened the door to the stable and went inside. 'Hello, my little lambs,' she called as Rudy and Rhonda trotted over for her to make a fuss of them. 'That's enough for you two,' she added firmly as they butted her legs with their hard heads. 'It's Fleet's turn today, he needs lots of attention.'

The tiny lamb was lying in the straw, his bent forelegs tucked awkwardly underneath him as he looked up at Mandy with huge liquid eyes. Mandy couldn't help feeling a pang of worry when she saw how thin he looked next to Rudy and Rhonda. She knelt down in the straw beside Fleet and began to massage and bend his ankles. He didn't seem to mind at all, just watched curiously as she gently worked the tendons. After a while, Mandy picked him up and lowered him to the ground. Fleet's legs dangled straight down like a normal lamb, until they touched the floor. Then they buckled weakly under him. Mandy lifted him up again and tried holding him so that his hooves were just flat on the ground, with no pressure on them at all.

'Dora's left a note to say that Rebecca let Fleet suckle again this morning, so she only gave him some goat's milk at lunchtime,' James said from the doorway.

'Brilliant,' Mandy replied without looking up,

intent on her work with the lamb. 'I'll do this for
a bit longer, then we can feed him and then do a
bit more.'

'I'll have a go if you like,' James offered.

'You take over and I'll get the bottle ready,'
Mandy decided. 'We mustn't wear him out,
though.'

It was dusk by the time they left but they were
very satisfied with Fleet's progress. 'He really did
put a bit of weight on his hooves at the end, didn't
he, James?' Mandy was jubilant. 'Tell me I didn't
imagine it!'

'You didn't imagine it,' James laughed. 'His legs seemed much stronger. And all that flexing is definitely loosening up his tendons. If he carries on at this rate, he'll be walking soon.'

'Wouldn't that be good?' said Mandy. 'I can hardly wait until tomorrow to do some more.'

But over the next few days, despite all their work, Fleet still didn't seem able to support his own weight. On Friday evening, Dora came in to see how they were getting on.

'I can't understand it,' Mandy protested. 'He was doing so well to begin with, and now, *nothing* seems to improve him.'

'That may be as good as it gets,' Dora said in a matter of fact voice. She bent down and felt Fleet's forelegs. 'They'll never bear his weight like that, little though he is. He's got a good way to go yet.' She looked at Mandy and James. 'If he gets there at all.'

Mandy's heart sank. Fleet was gazing up at her with big, trusting eyes. She couldn't let him down now, not after coming this far with him. 'But what else can we do?' she begged Dora. 'We're doing everything that Mum told us to, and it's not working any more.'

'I'm a sheep-farmer, Mandy,' Dora reminded her. 'I can't have time for sentiment. If he's not going to make the grade . . .' She stood up and shrugged. 'Give it the weekend and then we'll see.'

'We'll see what?' James echoed darkly when Dora had left.

'Don't even think about it,' Mandy groaned. 'Somehow, we've got to get Fleet on his feet.'

By the time she got home she was so exhausted she almost fell asleep at the table.

'Why so tired, Mandy? Is all this work getting too much for you?' asked Emily Hope, putting a slice of quiche on Mandy's plate. 'At least it's Friday today and you'll have the weekend to catch up.'

Suddenly Mandy found it hard to swallow. *The weekend.* That could be all the time Fleet had left. 'Mum, it's all gone wrong!' she declared, feeling her voice wobble.

'Why? What's happened?' Emily Hope sat down beside Mandy and put a comforting arm round her shoulders. 'It was all going so well, wasn't it?'

'Up till now,' Mandy said weakly. 'Tonight, Dora

said Fleet's legs might never get better and she's given us the weekend before she makes a decision about him.'

'That's not very long.' Adam Hope had come in from the study and heard the tale.

'You have to remember that sheep farming is Dora's livelihood,' Mrs Hope said gently. 'She has to be practical.'

'But surely having another lamb in the flock is good news?' Mandy said, bunching her hands into fists with frustration.

'Not if he can't walk,' said Mr Hope. 'But don't give up yet, things can turn round pretty quickly in an animal's life.'

'That's why you're so tired,' her mum added. 'It's not the work, it's the worry. There's nothing guaranteed to wear you down more quickly. Try to be positive, love. Remember, you and James are doing your very best for Fleet, and nobody could do more than that.'

'But will it be enough?' Mandy blurted out, still feeling troubled.

'Only you can answer that question,' Emily Hope said gently.

Mandy thought for a second. 'Then it *will* be enough,' she declared with a firm nod. 'We *will* get Fleet to walk, whatever it takes.'

'That's my girl,' said Adam Hope.

'Dad, there's another thing I want to ask you,' Mandy said, suddenly remembering. 'We called in on Lydia this afternoon, and she said that some men had been prowling around recently. And they came back again this morning, creeping around on her land. She's really frightened now, not surprisingly seeing as she's all alone up there.'

'I'll pop up tomorrow after morning surgery and see if I can find out what's going on,' said her dad, looking concerned.

'Thanks, Dad,' said Mandy. 'She'll appreciate it.'

'Why don't you have an early night, Mandy?' her mum suggested. 'It will do you good and things always look better in the morning. What time are you meeting James?'

'Half past seven!' Mandy rolled her eyes. 'But you know James, he hates getting up in the mornings. I hope he's on time.'

'You go up then, love,' said Mrs Hope. 'I'll bring you up a hot drink.'

* * *

Her mum had been right, Mandy thought to herself when she woke up the next morning. She did feel better after a good night's sleep. She yawned and stretched in bed, and looked at her watch. It was seven o'clock. Mandy sprang out of bed and dressed. Tapping softly on her parents' door she opened it and peeked in. 'It's only me,' she told them. 'I'm off now.'

'What about breakfast?' grunted Adam Hope, opening one eye.

'I'm not hungry,' Mandy answered.

'Well, take an apple or a banana,' Emily Hope reminded her. 'You can't work all day on an empty stomach.'

'OK,' Mandy agreed, turning to go.

'Oh, and Mandy,' her dad called out after her, 'good luck with Fleet.'

'Thanks,' Mandy said. 'I think we'll need it.'

Grabbing an apple from the bowl, she let herself out of the back door and collected her bike. She was five minutes early when she reached James's house. She ate her apple and waited. At exactly half past seven she heard the crunch of gravel and James came round the side of the house pushing his bike.

'James!' Mandy declared in mock horror. 'You're on time. Are you really awake?'

'Only just,' James admitted. 'It felt like I was getting up in the middle of the night.'

There was hardly any traffic on the road. But as they rode up the stony track to Lydia's farm, Mandy slammed on her brakes and came to an abrupt halt.

'What's wrong?' James asked, almost crashing into her.

'Shhh, look,' Mandy hissed. 'See? Up there, by the dead tree, in the passing space.'

'It's the car, isn't it?' James confirmed. 'The green estate that Lydia saw.'

'The burglars' car!' Mandy said. 'So they're back.'

'What shall we do?' asked James.

'We've got to go up there,' Mandy said. 'I don't think we should confront them, but we might be able to find out what they're up to.'

With James hot on her heels, Mandy cycled as fast as she could to the top of the track. They left their bicycles on the verge and carried on on foot. Soon the house was ahead of them and Houdini's field to their left.

Mandy stared in horror. 'James!' she gasped. 'The gate's wide open. He's gone, Houdini's gone!'

They raced across the courtyard. But before they could reach the house, Mandy heard a cry and she froze to the spot. She felt her scalp prickling as it came again, faint but definite from the barn.

'*Help, please somebody help*!'

It was a man's voice.

Mandy's head spun. Who could be in trouble?

Seven

Squaring their shoulders, Mandy and James walked over to the barn. The door was ajar. Mandy took a deep breath and with her heart pounding was about to step inside when another noise came from inside the barn – a loud tapping sound followed by muffled snorts.

'Come on, James,' Mandy said. 'We've got to go in.'

The sweet smell of hay hit her immediately. After the bright sunlight, Mandy couldn't see anything until her eyes adjusted to the gloom.

'Lydia,' she called urgently. 'Are you in here?'

'Help!' A voice came from above. 'Please, help us.' But it wasn't Lydia. It was the man's voice again.

Mandy and James walked into the middle of the barn and looked round. With a shock, Mandy realised that there were two men hiding behind the bales up in the hayloft, which extended across half the barn like a minstrels' gallery. And underneath, keeping them prisoner, was Houdini. The beautiful black goat stood in the middle of the floor, looking up at the hayloft with a very determined look in his eyes.

'Please,' one of the men pleaded. 'We've been here for hours; he won't let us out.'

'You can just stay up there,' Mandy said angrily, putting her arm round Houdini and smoothing his head. 'The police are on their way,' she bluffed. 'And my dad will be here very soon. What have you done with Lydia?'

'We haven't done anything with her,' said the other man, standing up and peering down at her. He had long hair, like Lydia had described. 'We were just crossing a field when that creature chased us. It's really dangerous!'

'We only just managed to escape! It was terrifying,' agreed the first man. He was shorter than his friend, and his eyes were huge with alarm.

'Well, you should have thought of that,' Mandy said indignantly, glaring up at them. 'Before you came to burgle a goat farm!'

'Burgle?' the long-haired man spluttered. 'What are you talking about? We're not burglars.'

'Then why have you been hanging around here?' James demanded bravely. 'Lydia's seen you more than once.'

'You've frightened the life out of Lydia,' Mandy added.

'I'm really sorry if we've frightened anyone,' said the long-haired man. 'My name's Tim and I'm a photographer, and this is Chris. He's a journalist.'

'We're here to do a piece about Miss Fawcett and the goats for the local paper, but we've never managed to meet her,' Chris explained. 'We've knocked on the door a couple of times but she always seems to be out.'

'That's why we came early this morning,' said Tim. 'And then that big goat came after us. I tell you, I've never run so fast in my life.'

Chris fumbled in the top pocket of his shirt and fished out a card. 'Look,' he said to Mandy. 'Here's my press card.'

Before Mandy could call out a warning, he threw it down. Houdini scooped up the small cardboard square with his tongue, chewed it a couple of times, and swallowed it.

'Oh dear,' Chris said in a surprised voice. 'Does it always do things like that?'

'*It* is a he,' Mandy told him. 'And his name is Houdini, and he does tend to be . . .' She searched for a word.

'A bit of a nibbler,' James supplied.

'That's right,' Mandy agreed. 'If you come down, I'll introduce you to him, and to Lydia. She's definitely in today.'

'Could you, er, put it, sorry *him*, I mean, Houdini, away and then we can meet Lydia?' Tim said nervously.

'Why don't you come down?' Mandy urged them. 'Come on, he's a super goat.'

'A goat with character,' James added proudly, patting Houdini's flank.

'A goat with attitude, more like!' muttered Tim.

'Look,' said Chris, with an anxious edge to his voice. 'We're not really country people, and to be honest, we're not that keen on meeting the goat. We'd be a lot happier if you put him back in his cage.'

'Cage?' Mandy laughed. 'Houdini doesn't live in a cage. He lives in that field where you first met him. But all right, we'll put him back.' She turned and led Houdini out of the barn without even looking at James, who was walking on Houdini's other side. When they were out of the barn, Mandy shut the door and collapsed in fits of laughter. 'You dangerous goat,' she joked, putting her arms around Houdini's neck and giving him a big hug.

James was laughing so much that he had to lean against the barn. 'Oh, Mandy,' he gasped, 'that would have made a good article for the local paper, wouldn't it?'

That set Mandy off again. 'Yes – local reporters held hostage by fierce goat!' Shoulders shaking with mirth, they led Houdini back to his field. 'Fancy thinking he was kept in a cage!' Mandy added, raising her eyebrows at James as she firmly shut the gate.

Chris and Tim were standing outside the barn brushing the straw from their clothes when Mandy and James returned. Tim had a bag slung over his shoulder, bulging with cameras and lenses. Chris had a clipboard with a notebook and pencil attached to it. He put out his hand to shake theirs. Mandy tried not to smile too broadly as she shook hands with them both, then turned and went to knock on Lydia's front door.

'And so you see they're journalists,' Mandy said, as she finished explaining to Lydia, who had opened the front door eventually and allowed them into her tiny, cluttered kitchen. 'And they want to interview you.'

'I'm perfectly happy to be interviewed,' said Lydia. 'But why didn't they simply knock on the door and ask in the first place?'

'Actually they did,' Mandy reminded her. 'But you wouldn't open it, remember?'

'Well, if people will go round looking like burglars,' Lydia said in a reasonable voice, 'then they can't expect people to open their doors, can they?'

Mandy had to stop herself from saying that

burglars didn't usually knock on the door. She caught James's eye, and guessed that he was thinking the same thing.

As Lydia sat down in a chair, Chris turned to a clean page of his notebook while Tim busily changed the lens on his camera. 'So how long have your goats been organic?' Chris began.

'Why, always, of course,' replied Lydia. 'I just use the same methods as my old dad did, and his dad before him.'

Chris raised his eyebrows, and scribbled some notes. 'And who puts the milk in the cartons and makes the cheese?' he asked. 'How many people work for you?'

'Nobody works for me, young man,' Lydia declared. 'I do it all myself. However, I have to tell you that none of my success with selling milk and cheese would have happened without my friends, Mandy and James. They set the whole thing up, and changed my life.'

'OK, Mandy and James,' said Tim, pointing his camera at them. 'Let's have you in the picture, too. Can you squeeze closer to Lydia please?'

Mandy stood on one side of Lydia, James stood on the other.

'Say cheese,' said Tim, laughing at his joke.

'Cheese!' chimed Mandy, James and Lydia as the camera flashed.

'Would we be able to see your herd?' asked Chris. 'Not too close mind, perhaps just from the doorway.'

'Certainly,' Lydia agreed. 'They're all in separate pens ready for milking so they won't give you any trouble.'

'And are they happier, your goats, being organic, I mean?' asked Tim, winding on his film. 'Do they realise what a nice life they have here?'

'Well, let's go over to the milking shed,' Lydia said drily, rolling her eyes at Mandy. 'And you can ask them yourself.'

Mandy looked at her watch. They should be getting over to Syke Farm now. Fleet would be waiting for them. 'Lydia, we must go,' she said, catching hold of her friend's sleeve as she set off towards the milking pen. 'James and I have got an important job to do at Syke Farm.'

'Very well, Mandy,' said Lydia. 'Thank you for

coming and sorting it all out for me. Don't forget
to take some more milk with you for that lamb.
Now, I'll show these nice young men my herd.
They'll enjoy that, won't they?'

Mandy grinned back at her. She had the feeling
that Chris and Tim would know a lot more about
goats by the time Lydia was finished with them.
*But I bet that little incident with Houdini won't be
mentioned in the article*, she thought to herself.

Eight

'We forgot to ask when the piece about Lydia would be in the paper,' puffed James, as they cycled up the lane that wound across the moor to Dora's farm.

'Jean always gets a copy to put in the waiting room,' Mandy told him. 'We're bound to see it. That reminds me, I must phone Dad and tell him he needn't worry about visiting Lydia now.'

'I'll get straight to work on Fleet,' said James, when they arrived at the farm gate. 'At least we've got all day today.'

'We've got to get him to make some progress, James,' said Mandy, her voice firm and positive.

They propped their bikes against the wall and Mandy went and knocked on the farmhouse door. There was no answer, so Mandy opened the door and let herself in. She wondered if Dora, Ken and Charlie had been up all night with the sheep and were catching up on sleep. Putting some of the goat's milk in the fridge and keeping one carton to give Fleet now, she went out into the hall where the phone hung on the wall by the front door. She didn't think Dora would mind if she made a quick call to her dad.

'Good morning, Animal Ark Veterinary Practice,' her dad announced. 'Adam Hope speaking, how may I help you?'

'Dad!' Mandy said, laughing. 'It's me!'

'Hello, love, what can I do for you?' he asked.

'I'm just phoning to say you don't need to visit Lydia,' Mandy said, and told him the story. By the time she'd finished, Mr Hope was roaring with laughter.

'That is something I would love to have seen,' he said. 'Whatever will Houdini get up to next?'

'I'd better go Dad, I'm using Dora's phone,' Mandy remembered.

'Hang on, there was something else,' Mr Hope said. 'Harry Wainwright needs another tub of powder for his bird's claw. I was planning to drop some off on my way to Lydia's, but now I won't be going.'

'I'll go when I get back,' Mandy said eagerly. 'I'd like to see if any more pigeons have come back yet.'

'Thanks, love,' said Mr Hope. 'I'll see you later.'

'See you, Dad,' said Mandy, replacing the phone. She crossed the yard to Rebecca's stable, opened the door and went inside. Rebecca was lying against the far wall with Rudy and Rhonda snuggled up beside her. Sitting on the floor beside her, James was gently massaging Fleet's foot. All three lambs lifted their heads when Mandy came in. She dropped to her knees by the door and called a greeting. Rudy and Rhonda immediately gambolled over, bumping into each other as they vied for her attention, each trying to scramble into her arms. Suddenly, Mandy heard James cry out.

'Mandy! Look at Fleet!' James's face was lit up with excitement as the lamb struggled vigorously in his arms. 'He feels really strong today.'

'Put him down on the ground,' Mandy said, trying to keep her voice level to hide her excitement. This was the first time Fleet had ever shown any enthusiasm for walking around.

But as James gently lowered the lamb to the ground, the little creature's legs collapsed under him, just as they always had. Mandy felt her optimism dwindle away.

She didn't know why, but she'd had a funny feeling that this time would be different. She looked at James and saw his excitement had been replaced by a look of disappointment just like hers.

'Oh, Fleet,' Mandy groaned. 'What are we going to do with you?'

As if he sensed her feelings, the lamb gave a loud bleat that brought Rebecca's head up sharply. Then he struggled valiantly to his feet, took three steps and collapsed on the floor in a heap. His forelegs were still bent, but they were straight enough to let the tips of his hooves touch the ground.

Mandy stared at him. 'He can do it, James!' she said in amazement. 'He can walk on his own.'

As if to prove it, Fleet gave another bleat, stood up and staggered across to flop on to Mandy's lap. Speechless with delight, Mandy buried her face in his soft woolly side.

'He didn't want to be left out,' Charlie said from the doorway. Mandy jumped. She hadn't notived him arrive. 'He was jealous of these two, I reckon.' Charlie went on, pointing to Rudy and Rhonda. 'The little chap's turned the corner, all

right. He'll come on in leaps and bounds now, you mark my words.' He shook his head. 'To be honest, I never thought he'd make it, after all this time. And I *still* can't get over that ewe taking him on.'

As he spoke, Rebecca limped over and nudged her two lambs out of the way, then pushed Fleet to his feet with her muzzle. Mandy felt sure she was encouraging him to walk. As the ewe hobbled awkwardly round the stable, Fleet stumbled after her, bleating loudly. Mandy breathed a huge sigh of relief. Rebecca's three-legged shuffle matched Fleet's pace exactly.

'She's walking well on that leg now, putting much more weight on it,' said Charlie, indicating Rebecca. 'If I get you some more cotton wool from the house, could you pad out the top of the splint for her, so it won't dig into her?'

'I'll come with you,' Mandy offered. 'I want to tell Dora about Fleet.'

'That's what I was coming to next,' said Charlie, tipping his cap back and scratching his head. 'Ken's had to take Dora into town; she's been up most of the night with a raging toothache. She didn't want to go, so he practically had to drag her to the dentist.'

'But there's nothing to be scared of,' Mandy said.

'That's Dora for you,' Charlie grinned. 'Anyhow, what I wondered was, as I've got so behind, could you two go up to the big field after lunch, and check the ewes for me? You could do a head count of the lambs, too. If you make sure everyone's thriving and none are in trouble, that would be a real help.'

'Of course we will,' Mandy said. 'We can stay and help all day if you like.'

'We expected to be here all day working on Fleet anyway,' James added, his eyes shining behind his spectacles. 'But thank goodness, he doesn't need us any more.'

'That would be great,' said Charlie. 'Now, let's get that cotton wool.'

When Mandy returned with the bag of cotton wool, James had begun cleaning out the stable. Mandy went across to the barn and fetched some more straw and then when it was clean and comfortable for the sheep, she started to pad Rebecca's splint.

The ewe stood quietly as Mandy gently tucked more cotton wool round the top of the piece of piping, pushing it down as much as she could so it wouldn't fall out. 'She's very good, isn't she?' Mandy remarked. 'There's not many sheep who would put up with so much fussing.'

'She's great,' James agreed. 'She's done a fantastic job with Fleet.'

Mandy sat back on her heels and watched the lamb trotting unevenly after his adopted brother and sister. 'It's as if now that he's finally found his feet, he can't keep off them,' Mandy said, feeling a warm sense of contentment bubbling up inside her. 'I was so worried last night that this wouldn't happen, and that he'd never be able to walk. Now look at him.'

'His legs should begin to get bigger and stronger on their own, as he uses them more,' said James.

'Yes, I think you're right,' Mandy said, smiling at him.

By the time they had fed Fleet, it was time for their own lunch. They washed their hands under the outside tap in the yard, then went over to the house. On the table in the kitchen, Charlie had set out thick slices of brown bread spread with butter, a large chunk of cheddar cheese and a bowl of tomatoes.

'Help yourselves,' he said, pointing at the plates on the pine dresser. 'There's pickle here, too.'

Until that moment, Mandy hadn't realised how hungry she was. It seemed a long time since she'd eaten her breakfast apple. When they'd finished, Charlie fetched a cake from the larder and cut them all a slice of rich, sticky parkin.

'Mmm, this is delicious,' said James, licking his fingers.

'It is, isn't it?' Mandy agreed. 'It tastes as good as my gran's, and that's saying something! Did Dora make it?' she asked Charlie.

'No, she bought it at the W.I. sale yesterday,' he said, cutting himself another slice. 'When she popped into Welford.'

'Then it probably *is* my gran's parkin!' said Mandy. 'She always makes some for the sale.'

After lunch, they collected their helmets ready for the quad bike and with James driving, they rode carefully up to the lambing field. The field was big, almost four acres, and sheep were dotted about in little groups. They scattered in alarm when James drove too close, which made counting difficult.

'Let's drive to the far end and work our way round the edges,' Mandy suggested.

'Right, I'll stop halfway and you can have a drive,' said James.

'That's OK,' Mandy said, feeling very generous. 'You drive, I'll count.'

By the time they'd driven around the whole field, Mandy had counted sixty-seven lambs and eleven ewes still to lamb. They entered the details in the record book as Charlie had shown them.

'That's fourteen more lambs than yesterday!' Mandy said in amazement. 'I'm not surprised Charlie's worn out.'

'Dora's flock is pretty big now with the ones in the lower field, as well,' James remarked. 'There'll be a lot of wool come shearing time.'

'I wonder if Mum set anything up with Dora for Gran's knitting circle?' Mandy mused. 'I was so worried about Fleet that I forgot to ask.'

'Well, we can ask her tonight,' said James. 'Come on, we'd better get going.'

'Do you need us for anything more?' Mandy asked Charlie when they got back to the yard.

'No, that's OK. You can head off now and thanks very much for all you've done,' he replied, nodding gratefully to them. 'I'll tell Dora how well that little-un's doing, don't worry.'

'Thanks,' said Mandy, feeling as if a big weight had been lifted off her shoulders.

'I promised Dad I'd take some antibiotic powder over to Harry when we get home,' she called to James as they cycled out of the yard. 'Want to come?'

'Yes, definitely, I'd really like to see where he trains the birds,' said James. 'Can we call in at my house on the way to let Mum know?'

'Of course,' Mandy said. 'We can take Blackie.' She knew that James's black Labrador loved coming out to run beside their bikes. They hadn't been able to take him to Syke Farm because of all the sheep, but Mandy didn't want him to feel left out.

Their tyres crunched on the gravel drive as they rode round the back of James's house. Almost immediately the back door opened and

James's mother came out to greet them.

'I just called in to say I'm going out again,' James explained to his mum.

'I don't think so, James,' said Mrs Hunter, and Mandy noticed a smile twitching at her lips. 'You have a major dog bathing job to do.'

'Why?' James asked, concerned. 'Where's Blackie? What's happened?'

'I've banished him to the very bottom of the garden,' said Mrs Hunter. 'He's even grubbier than usual, I'm afraid.'

James called his dog, but instead of his usual boisterous welcome, Blackie slunk up the garden with his tail between his legs.

'Blackie!' James blurted out in stunned disbelief. 'What have you done?'

The Labrador that stood before them wasn't a glossy black dog anymore. His whole body was caked in cream-coloured mud.

'Yuk,' said James, as the strong smell of manure drifted up.

'Now you see why I wouldn't have him in the house!' said James's mother. 'I felt sorry for him and took him for a walk. And what does he do to

repay this favour?' She raised her eyebrows at
them. 'First he went for a swim in the river, then
he rolled in the dust on the bank. And as if that
wasn't enough, his skin must have itched when it
dried, so he tried to scratch his back by rolling in
the lane, just after the cows had been through.'

'Oh, Blackie.' Mandy sighed, looking at the
dog's mournful eyes. 'You are a mess. I'd offer to
help you, James, but I've got to take that powder
to Harry.'

James pulled a face and nodded. 'Come on,
boy,' he called to Blackie.

'Here we are, James,' Mrs Hunter added,
holding out something to him and winking at
Mandy, 'This might help.'

'A peg?' James raised his eyebrows. 'What for?'

'To put on your nose, of course!' Mandy called,
as she cycled away.

Nine

'That's excellent news about Fleet,' said Adam Hope, as he delved into the medicine cupboard in the Animal Ark surgery. 'You and James should feel very proud of yourselves. Now, here you are,' he went on, handing Mandy the small plastic tub that contained the antibiotic powder. 'Mr Wainwright lives in one of those cottages up near Monkton Spinney. It's not far, and shouldn't take you long on your bike.'

Armed with Harry's address and the medication for the pigeon's claw, Mandy cycled peacefully along in the early evening sunshine, past the village green and down the winding lane that led out of the village towards the small wood that was called Monkton Spinney. Just before the lane wound under the trees, there were two small cottages that lay back from the road. The last of the crocuses carpeted a wide grassy verge in front of them.

Mandy leaned her bike against the hedge belonging to Dove Cottage, walked up the path and knocked on the blue front door.

'Mandy!' exclaimed Harry when he opened the door. 'Come in, come in.'

'I've brought you the antibiotic powder,' she said, handing him the packet.

'That's very kind of you.' He bustled along the hallway. 'Follow me, I've just made some hot chocolate. Would you like some?'

'Yes, please,' Mandy replied.

The kitchen was neat and tidy with red checked curtains and a small round table with a matching check tablecloth. A pan bubbled gently on the stove.

'I wasn't expecting a guest, but there's plenty

for two,' said Harry. He stirred the chocolate and poured it into two red mugs, handing one to Mandy. 'Now that you're here, would you like to see my birds?' he asked. 'They've been a great comfort to me since my wife died.'

'Yes, I'd love to. Has Super Sam come back yet?' Mandy asked, sipping her drink. 'Thanks, this is delicious,' she added.

'Good, I'm glad you like it, and no, he hasn't,' Harry said, shrugging his shoulders. 'I'm beginning to wonder if he'll ever come back.'

'Try and stay positive, sometimes things get better even when you don't expect them to,' Mandy said, and told him all about Fleet.

'That lamb has a lot to be grateful to you for,' Harry remarked. He stood up and took a key from a hook by the door. 'Shall we make a visit to the pigeon loft, now?' he said, opening the back door.

'The loft?' Mandy echoed. 'In the garden? I thought a loft would be at the top of the house, under the roof?'

'They were originally,' Harry explained. 'Years ago, people kept their birds in the highest place in the house, like the loft, to keep them safe from poachers. But then the poachers started paying small boys to climb up and steal them.'

'I didn't realise they were that valuable,' Mandy admitted, as she followed him down a narrow stone path to the back of the garden.

'They always have been. People will pay a lot of money for a pedigree bird,' Harry told her. 'Especially one like Super Sam. He was bred from a Golden Pair, that's the best there is. Now, there's my loft.' He stopped and held out one arm with pride.

Mandy stared in amazement at the wooden structure ahead of her. 'That's not a pigeon loft!' she exclaimed. 'That's a pigeon palace!' The loft was the size of a large garden shed, spotlessly clean and beautifully made, with narrow glassless windows at the bottom for ventilation. It even had balconies where the birds could sit outside in the sunshine. It was obvious that Harry had only the very best for his birds.

'I made it all myself,' he informed her, beaming. 'Come inside.' He unlocked the door and ushered her in.

Inside, the loft was divided into three sections with sliding doors between them.

'Each of the sections are for different birds,' Harry explained. 'These are the young birds that came back after the accident,' he said, sliding the first door across and walking inside. Mandy followed him and he closed the door behind them. It was like standing in a very small garden shed. There were places where the birds could perch

next to each other, and each enclosed nest box had a neatly written record card beside it, giving details of the different birds.

'How many birds are in here?' Mandy asked, listening in delight to the soft cooing sounds all around her. The shed was warm and a bit stuffy, and smelled of feathers and grain.

'Eighteen,' Harry told her. 'All the young ones are back now, thank goodness. And there's one that I didn't take with me that day. I'm training her for a special race.'

Mandy could see now that all of the nest boxes contained a bird, all except one, right at the very top. 'Who lives there?' she asked.

'That's Super Sam's place,' Harry said with a sigh. 'I'd entered him in a big race next week, where they start off in France and have to fly nearly eight hundred miles home. He would've won it too, I'm certain he would.'

'That seems an awful long way for a pigeon to fly,' Mandy remarked. 'How do they find their way home?'

'I thought you might ask that,' said Harry with a grin. 'The thing is, nobody really knows.

Some experts think they navigate by the sun.'

'How do they decide who the winner is if they all fly home to their own lofts?' Mandy wondered out loud, puzzled by the idea of hundreds of birds arriving at different locations all over the country.

'Ah, they have a special method, so no one can cheat,' Harry explained. 'Each owner has a special clock and at the start of a race, our clocks are checked against the club's master clock. Then after a race as soon as our bird comes home we take the rubber tag off its leg and clock it in.'

'How do they get back inside the loft?' Mandy asked. 'Surely they don't fly straight in, do they?'

'They do indeed. Let's go outside and I'll show you,' said Harry, closing the partition door behind them.

'But the entrances look so small,' Mandy said gazing up at the round holes that Harry told her led straight into the nest boxes. 'Don't they bash their wings going in?'

'The entrances are designed so they won't hurt themselves,' said Harry. 'Especially as their wings can be sore after a long race. Pigeons are very clever birds, you know. They've been used for thousands of years to carry messages. In fact, in the Second World War, lots of pigeons even won the Dickin Medal.'

'What's the Dickin Medal?' Mandy asked.

'It's a bravery medal that was awarded to the pigeons for their heroic actions,' Harry told her. 'It's the animal version of the Victoria Cross.'

'Wow, that's fantastic,' Mandy said. She was already catching Harry's enthusiasm for his birds. 'Do they always fly straight home?'

'Usually,' Harry said, then smiled as if he was remembering something. 'One time, I put Super Sam in a race and I could tell he was feeling grumpy. But I'd clocked him in and I thought he'd snap out of it. But do you know what that bird did?'

'What?'

'At about the time he should have returned, I went to the loft with my clock and waited for him,' said Harry. 'Soon, I saw him coming back and I called him. But do you think he'd come down? No way! He flew round and round and then he settled in that tree, and just watched me. I couldn't take the rubber tag off his leg with him sitting up there in the tree and the minutes were ticking by.'

Mandy started to laugh. 'What did you do then?'

'I tell you, Mandy, I was tearing my hair out and jumping up and down with frustration,' said Harry, joining in her laughter. 'It sounds funny now, but at the time I called him all the names under the sun. It was an hour and a half before he finally came down to his nest box and let me take the tag off. An hour and a half wasted. We could have won that race, but I reckon he wanted to teach me a lesson.'

Mandy stared up at the sky, imagining Super Sam teasing Harry. She hadn't realised that pigeons could have such distinctive personalities, like a cat or dog. She tried to imagine a bird swooping down, coming home safely at last, to his home and owner. As she gazed up at the clouds, Mandy noticed a moving speck, way off in the distance. 'Look, Harry,' she said. 'Is that a bird?'

Harry frowned and studied the sky. 'It *is* a bird, Mandy!' He gasped suddenly and clenched his hands together as the speck drew closer and closer. 'It's him!' he exclaimed, his face breaking into a huge grin. 'I'm certain it is, it's Super Sam.'

Mandy found it hard to believe that Harry could recognise his pigeon at such a distance, but then she remembered that he must have watched that bird fly home many times before.

'Mandy, this is a wonderful day,' Harry beamed at her. 'I can't believe it's happened at last. He really *has* come home.'

They watched as the bird glided over the treetops and swooped gracefully downwards into the garden. In one swift movement, Super Sam folded his jet black wings and slipped through the entrance into his nest box.

'That's incredible,' said Mandy in an awed voice. 'He was absolutely sure of where he was going.'

'It's easy for him, he's a pigeon,' Harry said. 'Flying is what he does. After all, I don't expect you keep bumping into the doorframe when you walk through a door now, do you?'

'No,' Mandy agreed. She could see Harry's logic, but it still seemed incredible to her.

She followed Harry into the loft and watched as he lovingly picked the champion bird out of his nest box. Mandy had to admit he was a beautiful pigeon. His feathers were glossy and black, and his eyes were bright and knowing. She watched with interest as Harry held the bird's tail and feet in one hand and carefully spread its wings with the other, turning him this way and that to examine him for any sign of injury.

'He's fine,' said Harry at last. 'I don't know where he's been, but he's not damaged at all.' He kissed the top of Super Sam's head and gently stroked his breast feathers. 'So you've come home at last,' he said softly to the bird as he put him back in his nest box.

Then he reached into the nest box directly below it. 'This little one is Super Sam's daughter,' Harry announced, handing the pigeon to Mandy. 'With Sam gone I've not been able to concentrate on her training, but now he's back, I'll feel more like it. In fact, I think I'll put her in the French race instead of him, it'll be a wonderful chance for her to try her wings over the distance. I put a lot of store on this one.'

'She is gorgeous,' Mandy agreed, holding the bird the way she had seen Harry do it. The pigeon was black like her father but without the white flash on her face. Instead, she had two white feathers on each wing. 'What's her name?' Mandy asked. 'Is she Super Samantha?'

Harry laughed. 'I've been calling her Baby Sam but she needs a proper name for racing.' He watched Mandy with the bird. 'But you've brought me such luck today with Sam coming back that I'd like to name her after you.'

'Me!' Mandy exclaimed.

'Yes, you!' Harry nodded. 'Now, how about Lucky Mandy?'

Mandy wrinkled her nose. 'It's nice, but it doesn't have the same ring as Super Sam, does it?'

Harry thought for a moment then smiled. 'I think I've got it,' he said. 'From today,' he stroked the bird's head, 'her name will be Magic Mandy!'

Ten

Mandy felt a warm glow of satisfaction as she cycled back to Welford. Everything had worked out perfectly in the end. She planned to carry on visiting Rebecca and her family at Syke Farm, but things could get back to normal now. Though she'd loved being involved with the lambing, Mandy had really missed helping out at Animal Ark after school.

'Guess what?' she said, as she walked into the kitchen and sat down at the table.

'I give in,' said Mrs Hope, lowering the

newspaper. 'We've been so busy without you that I haven't the energy even to try.'

'Harry's champion bird has come back and . . .' Mandy hesitated to add more drama, 'he's named his next best bird Magic Mandy after me!'

'Goodness me!' said Mr Hope, as he drizzled dressing on a bowl of salad. 'That's very nice of him. Perhaps you'll win races and become famous.'

'Actually, she's in a race next week,' Mandy said. 'Dad, I was wondering, how long will it be before Rebecca and her family can go outside again? They must be getting a bit fed up being indoors all the time.'

'Soon, I should think,' replied her dad. 'She's walking well on that leg, you say?'

'Yep,' Mandy answered. 'Charlie thought so, too.'

'Well, we'll give her a few more days and then decide,' said Adam Hope.

Early the following Wednesday morning, the phone rang just as Mandy was setting off for school. She picked it up to hear Dora on the other end.

'There's nothing wrong is there?' Mandy asked, suddenly feeling worried.

'No, the sheep are all fine, but they're getting restless now,' replied Dora. 'That's why I want to speak to your dad. Every time I pass the stable Rebecca grumbles at me, and the lambs are getting very fed up of being cooped up. It's time they felt grass under their feet.'

'Good, I'll just get him,' Mandy said, and called loudly, 'Dad, it's Dora for you.'

Mandy looked at her watch. She knew she should leave immediately as James would be waiting for her, but she wanted to hear her dad's reply.

'Dora,' Adam Hope answered the phone. 'What can I do for you this beautiful morning?' He listened as Dora explained. 'I would say I'd come and check them over after morning surgery, but someone is hovering around me like a butterfly, looking very anxious indeed,' said Mr Hope, glancing sideways at Mandy. 'I think we'd better make it after school, when Mandy and James can both come and see the result of their efforts, if that's OK with you.'

'Brilliant! Thanks, Dad,' Mandy said as he put down the phone. Then she raced off to collect her bike. 'See you later,' she called.

James was looking at his watch as Mandy sped up to him.

'Sorry I'm late, but I've got some good news,' she said, breathlessly relaying Dora's conversation with her dad. 'We're going up there after school. I can't wait to see Fleet put his feet on grass for the first time and run free. Well, more like hobble free really,' she finished with a grin. She knew it would be a while before Fleet's legs were properly straight, but as long as he wasn't in pain and could run around, Mandy didn't mind too much.

'And Rudy and Rhonda too,' James reminded her. 'They've never trodden on grass either.'

'You're right,' Mandy said. 'Because they're bigger than Fleet I wasn't thinking about them. But they're the ones who started all this off, by being born in the lane!'

Mandy found it hard to concentrate during lessons that day and was told off twice for fidgeting. When the final bell rang, she met up with James in the playground and they cycled back to Welford as fast as they could.

'We'll pick you up in a few minutes,' Mandy called to James, as she turned down the road that led to Animal Ark. 'As soon as I've changed.'

'Mum's coming as well,' her dad told her when she rushed breathlessly into the kitchen. 'She didn't want to miss the liberation of the lambs!'

'I bet they'll love it, being free I mean,' Mandy said, pounding up the stairs two at a time.

'I should think Rebecca will be glad to be outside again,' said Emily Hope. 'What tough little animals hill sheep are!'

James was waiting outside his house when the Land-rover arrived and they set off for Syke Farm.

'How will we get them all up to the lambing field?' Mandy wondered aloud.

'It will probably be best to use the trailer,' Adam Hope suggested. 'It's not far, but it might be asking a bit much for their legs so soon. Dora will know what to do.'

Mandy felt a surge of excitement as they drove into the yard. Dora was already there with the tractor and trailer. Mandy waited patiently while her dad examined the sheep and finally pronounced them fit and healthy.

'Fleet!' she exclaimed as he bounced up to her through the straw. 'You look terrific.'

'He's put on weight since Saturday,' James declared.

'And look how well he's walking,' Mandy observed. 'Charlie said he'd come on in leaps and bounds, and he has!'

'Rebecca's leg is healing well,' Mr Hope added. 'She'll need to keep the splint on for another few weeks, but I don't see any reason why these animals can't go out right now.'

James lowered the back of the trailer and Mandy led Rebecca out of the stable, steering her by clutching a handful of thick wool on her neck. Rudy and Rhonda followed their mum happily up the ramp but Fleet had a great deal of trouble when his poor crooked hooves first touched the concrete. He slipped and slithered around, and the other two lambs, thinking it was a game, came skittering back down the ramp to join in, while Rebecca watched from inside the trailer.

'Catch them!' Dora called. 'They're getting over-

excited. We don't want another broken leg.'

Dora managed to grab Rudy and Mandy got hold of Fleet. Mr Hope made a valiant attempt to catch Rhonda but she wriggled out of his grip.

'Can you try and catch her, James?' called Mr Hope as the lamb shot between his feet. 'Oh, well caught,' he said as James dived to his left like a goalkeeper and captured runaway Rhonda.

'I think you two had better travel in the trailer with them,' Emily Hope suggested. 'It might be safer for those lambs if they don't run around too much in there.'

With Fleet at her feet and Rudy under one arm, Mandy sat in the trailer while Dora hitched it to the tractor. James hung on to Rhonda, who wriggled like a mad thing and bleated crossly. With the Land-rover following behind, Dora drove carefully out of the yard, along the lane and up the hill to the lambing field.

Ken and Charlie were waiting to open the gate for the little convoy. Mandy and James waited as Dora lowered the ramp of the trailer.

'I want to see the moment when Fleet feels the

grass,' Mandy said, giving Fleet one last pat and jumping out.

'That's right, Mandy,' said Adam Hope. 'Let's leave them to come out on their own, if we can.'

Rebecca hobbled to the edge of the trailer and stood at the top of the ramp, her lambs gathering around her. She refused to budge.

'Come on, Rebecca,' Mandy urged. 'What's the matter?'

'She probably doesn't feel safe coming down the ramp with that leg,' Adam Hope said. 'You'll have to jump up and give her a bit of support, stop her sliding.'

Climbing back into the trailer, Mandy put her arms around Rebecca's middle and carefully supported her weight. Step by uneven step she helped the sheep down the ramp until she was safely on the grass. As soon as she was on firm ground, Rebecca bleated happily to her lambs, as if she was telling them to come out too.

Rudy and Rhonda trotted down the ramp at once and began jumping around in little circles. Rebecca watched them carefully.

'Do you think she'll abandon Fleet now?' Mandy voiced her thoughts out loud.

'Or will his real mum want him back?' James asked. 'Now that he's well again?'

'Wait and see,' said Emily Hope. 'We need to give them all a chance to adjust to the outdoor life.'

Now the two lambs were racing round the field and Rebecca turned away from Fleet to follow them. The little lamb stood at the top of the ramp, gazing after his foster mother with enormous eyes.

'Don't leave him,' Mandy begged quietly. 'Please Rebecca, he still needs your help.'

Suddenly, Rebecca turned back and bleated at Fleet. He ran down the ramp, lost his footing halfway down and slid the rest of the way on his bottom. Mandy couldn't help laughing. Fleet stood up, sniffed the grass and looked at Mandy with a surprised expression on his face. He pawed the ground and tried an experimental jump. Rebecca hobbled over and gave him a gentle shove. Fleet stuck his head under her and began to suckle. Rebecca gave a contented sigh and dropped her head to nibble the grass.

'What are Rudy and Rhonda doing?' Mandy asked, shading her eyes with her hand and gazing over the vast field of sheep.

'They'll be back; they won't leave their mum yet awhile,' said Dora. 'They're just finding their feet and enjoying their first taste of freedom.'

'Do you think they will remember us?' Mandy wondered.

'Despite what people say, sheep are very intelligent, and they definitely remember things,' Dora said, nodding.

James pointed across the field. 'Look, Rudy and Rhonda are coming back!' The twin lambs scooted between the other ewes and raced over to join Fleet, shoved their heads firmly under Rebecca's belly and twitched their little tails with pleasure.

'I'm in your debt, Mandy Hope,' said Dora smiling down at the family scene. 'And you, James. I doubted you could do it, but you did. We're very grateful. Me and the sheep, and all of us.'

Mandy opened her mouth to say it was nothing when in the pocket of Adam Hope's coat, his phone began to ring. They were all silent as he answered it.

'Well, hello,' said Adam Hope, giving nothing away. 'She's actually standing beside me, do you want to have a word with her? Just a sec.'

Mandy expected him to pass the phone to her mum and she blinked in surprise when her dad handed it to her. 'Hello,' she said cautiously, wondering who it could be. 'Oh, hi, yes, what? That's wonderful. Thanks for ringing to let me know.' She switched the phone off and handed it back to her dad.

'Come on, Mandy, what's it all about?' said Mrs Hope. 'We're all itching to know.'

'That was Harry,' Mandy announced, her face breaking into a big smile. 'And guess what? Magic Mandy has just won her first race!'

STALLION IN THE STABLE
Animal Ark Holiday Special

Lucy Daniels

Animals always come first for Mandy Hope, and at Animal Ark – her parents' busy veterinary surgery – Mandy is always making new friends.

Mandy and James are really looking forward to their holiday at the Kincraig Trekking Centre. A whole week of riding in the beautiful Scottish Highlands! But the owner of the centre is worried about the Highland Pony stud on the other side of the mountain. It looks like the ponies are being mistreated. Then one of the stallions goes missing . . .

CAT IN THE CANDLELIGHT
Animal Ark Holiday Special

Lucy Daniels

Animals always come first for Mandy Hope, and at Animal Ark – her parents' busy veterinary surgery – Mandy is always making new friends.

Welford is in the grip of a flood when, late one night, Mandy rescues a cat washed to Animal Ark in an old barrel. Where can it have come from? Despite the weather, Mandy is determined to find a home for the little cat – and to arrange some seasonal celebrations that the village will never forget!